# The Queen, the Cambion, and Seven Others

# Conversation Pieces

A Small Paperback Series from Aqueduct Press
Subscriptions available: www.aqueductpress.com

## About the Aqueduct Press
## Conversation Pieces Series

The feminist engaged with sf is passionately interested in challenging the way things are, passionately determined to understand how everything works. It is my constant sense of our feminist-sf present as a grand conversation that enables me to trace its existence into the past and from there see its trajectory extending into our future. A genealogy for feminist sf would not constitute a chart depicting direct lineages but would offer us an ever-shifting, fluid mosaic, the individual tiles of which we will probably only ever partially access. What could be more in the spirit of feminist sf than to conceptualize a genealogy that explicitly manifests our own communities across not only space but also time?

Aqueduct's small paperback series, Conversation Pieces, aims to both document and facilitate the "grand conversation." The Conversation Pieces series presents a wide variety of texts, including short fiction (which may not always be sf and may not necessarily even be feminist), essays, speeches, manifestoes, poetry, interviews, correspondence, and group discussions. Many of the texts are reprinted material, but some are new. The grand conversation reaches at least as far back as Mary Shelley and extends, in our speculations and visions, into the continually-created future. In Jonathan Goldberg's words, "To look forward to the history that will be, one must look at and retell the history that has been told." And that is what Conversation Pieces is all about.

L. Timmel Duchamp

Jonathan Goldberg, "The History That Will Be" in Louise Fradenburg and Carla Freccero, eds., *Premodern Sexualities* (New York and London: Routledge, 1996)

Published by Aqueduct Press
PO Box 95787
Seattle, WA 98145-2787
www.aqueductpress.com

ISBN: 978-1-61976-028-8

"Seven Smiles and Seven Frowns" was published in *Lightspeed*, November 2012.

"The Cinnamon Cavalier" was published in *Fantasy Magazine*, April 2008.

"The Margay's Children" was published in *The Beastly Bride*, Viking Press 2010 (Datlow/Windling, eds.).

"The Progress of Solstice and Chance" was published in *Realms of Fantasy*, August 2011.

"The Bear Dresser's Secret" was published in *Electric Velocipede* 17/18, Spring 2009.

"Sir Morgravain Speaks of Night Dragons and Other Things" was published in *The Magazine of Fantasy and Science Fiction*, July/August 2011.

"The Queen and the Cambion" was published in *The Magazine of Fantasy and Science Fiction*, March/April 2012.

Cover illustration by Arthur Rackham from *The Sleeping Beauty* by C. S. Evans, William Heinemann, London, 1920.
All text illustrations were published before 1923 and are public domain in the United States of America.
Book Design by Kathryn Wilham
Original Block Print of Mary Shelley by Justin Kempton: www.writersmugs.com

Conversation Pieces
Volume 35

The Queen, the Cambion,

and Seven Others

by
Richard Bowes

*For Lee and Peter*

# Contents

Illustration by Arthur Rackham for *A Midsummer Night's Dream* by William Shakespeare, 1908

Myth is the sea on which the Fantasy story floats.
Legend is the wind that drives it.
Its place of birth is the Fairy Tale.

Illustration by Arthur Rackham for *A Midsummer Night's Dream* by William Shakespeare, 1908

# Seven Smiles and Seven Frowns

## 1.

Each time I find a new apprentice in these times of trouble I remember being a girl of twelve, getting close to thirteen. The other lads and maidens my age were already starting to pair off. But I was still taking my little brother and sister to hear the Witch of the Forest of Avalon tell stories on her porch on summer evenings. The old tales always held a fascination for me.

Our town was a peaceful one on the edge of the forest. In those days Bertrade was the Witch. Feet or a farm wagon are the only way ordinary people around here travel, and the Witch lived within walking distance. We'd gather in her yard in front of the huge tree.

The fine house was of wood and stone and even had glass windows, rare enough to seem like magic to me. The porch was laid out on the roots, and the windows looked out of the trunk. The front door would open, and the Witch, dressed not unlike our mothers but carrying a long, twisted grey stick, would appear and say, "Welcome to the Oak of Avalon." Then we'd all come up on the porch where lemonade and ginger cookies would suddenly appear on a table. The light ebbed as the telling progressed. At the story's end Bertrade would stand and tell us to hurry home, and we'd run barefoot through the gathering dark.

She told the old tales, ones I'd heard many times: the brother and sister lost in the forest, the dancing daughters, the scullery maid who's really a princess, the frightened dragon, and the forgetful witch. Bertrade always described that one as "an unusual wicked witch."

So familiar were those stories and so fine were her tellings that I mostly floated on their surfaces, like you do hearing a favorite song.

But she also told unusual ones. Especially late in the summer when dusk came earlier and the air might have a crisp tang. Some of these were rare, and a few were brand new to me. So they caught my full attention, made me wonder.

One evening right at the start she said, "This is a story that the Fairies tell." We'd heard many of these, and they were always about Fairies: wise Fairy godmothers, tricky but wonderful gifts, brave princes and beautiful princesses disguised as pigs and toads.

She looked directly at me before announcing the name of a story I'd never heard. "Seven Smiles and Six Frowns," she said. Then she started.

"One fine morning in early May, into a forest, much like the one in which we find ourselves, came Prince Alaric, eldest son of the King Who Rules.

"He rode a horse with wings and wore a crown, a cape, gloves, a sword, fine britches that fit into his boots. Prince Alaric was handsome and well-liked by all. He had about him a questing spirit and love of everything that was new and unknown.

"His parents, anxious to make a match, invited every princess in the neighborhood, each lovelier than the next, to balls and fêtes. But Alaric was satisfied with none of them.

"On the particular day of this story I tell, Prince Alaric was separated from his companions and found himself alone and deep in woods where he had never traveled before. He had no fear because the Fairy Folk had loved him since he was a child and had given him all manner of presents.

"Bellephron the winged horse, gift of the Lord of Day, would carry him above the trees. The cloak, a gift of the Lady of Night would make him invisible to his enemies. The ring given him by the Vizier of Wisdom enabled him to pass through solid walls. The sword from the Knight of Wands would smash the weapons of any foes. The boots from the Messenger of the Winds would carry him a thousand leagues in a single hour. The belt and britches from the Shining Maiden made him stronger than any hundred men.

"But the crown from the King Who Rules was the greatest gift of all. For that permitted him to see the minds of others."

Listening to "Seven Smiles" made me concentrate, question the list of what the prince wore. Like all fairy stories, this took place in a distant past. I'd never heard of the Shining Maiden or the Lord of the Day. But the King Beneath the Hill was and is the King Who Rules us.

I thought about the growing dusk, the chirping of birds settling down for the night, the smell of the wood

3

around me, the ginger cookies I could still taste, and the feel of the floorboards on my feet.

I realized the Witch had paused, and when I glanced up, she was looking my way, making sure she had my attention before starting again.

"As he rode through this woods Prince Alaric saw the most beautiful maiden he had ever seen standing in the forest clad only in a simple dress and seeming to be part of the leaves and trees."

And I imagined a woman standing in a fine green shift, barefoot. She was tall, and blended into the trees, and looked Alaric right in the eye. Sure now that I was with her, Bertrade continued.

"Then Alaric smiled the smile that had won the heart of each and every princess. But the Maiden only frowned the frown given her by the Nixie of the Silver Pond and said, 'Your horse gives me much displeasure.'

"So the prince dismounted, and when he did, the winged horse disappeared. Alaric smiled again but the maiden only frowned the frown she had learned from the Dryad of the Farthest Moors.

"'Your cloak gives me much displeasure,' she said. Alaric kept his smile, but unfastened the gold chain. The cloak, the gift of the Lady of the Night, fell to the ground and disappeared.

"The prince smiled but the Maiden said. 'Your ring gives me much displeasure,' and the Vizier of Wisdom's gift disappeared in the dirt of the road.

"So it went with the Prince smiling and the Maiden frowning the frown given her by the Gryphon of the Tall Mountain and saying, 'Your sword gives me much displeasure.' The Prince let the gift of the Knight of Wands fall to the ground and disappear.

"Still he smiled and the Maiden showed him the frown given her by the Sybil of the Iron Throne and said, 'Your boots give me much displeasure.' He stripped off the gift of the Messenger of the Winds, and they too disappeared and he stood barefoot.

"Thus it was that Prince Alaric smiled, and the Maiden only frowned her frown from the Harvest Queen and said, 'Your belt and britches give me great displeasure.' And he unbuckled the belt, stepped out of the britches and they disappeared."

We all giggled at the idea. But the Witch just paused then said, "At last he stood in just his crown and a simple shirt. Before the maiden could tell him the crown gave her great displeasure, he took it off. And without even using it to read the Maiden's mind he put the gift of the King Who Rules on the ground where it too disappeared.

"Then with no more to give than the poorest of the poor, Alaric smiled at the Maiden with all his love.

"And the Maiden was the Princess Gerathea of Astolot kept under a spell by the Witch of the Forest, one of those unusual wicked Witches. The spell would last until she found a man who would give up his crown for her. She had no more frowns left. Instead she smiled at the prince with the same love he had shown her.

"Then all the gifts Alaric had surrendered reappeared. The Prince lifted the Maiden up before him on his winged horse and together they flew back to the palace where they announced their betrothal and were wed amid their parents' blessing and the people's rejoicing."

5

## 2.

The ending gave me displeasure just as I knew it must have given Gerathea. As the younger children thanked Bertrade and got up to go home in the gathering darkness, the Witch of Avalon beckoned me close to her.

"If you were to come tomorrow evening you might well hear a tale you like better." I nodded, wide-eyed, and she added. "Tell no one but your parents."

And then because it was dark with a chill in the air and because the youngest children were a little afraid, the Witch of Avalon waved the long, gray stick she carried and a ball of fire appeared. It floated in the air in front of us on our way home and stopped at each gate until the children from that house were indoors.

Our house was last. I waited until my brother and sister were in bed before I told my parents what Bertrade told me. My father looked unsure, and my mother looked a bit sad, but both nodded agreement like they had known this would happen.

My parents were indulgent, never pressed me to behave like the other girls or asked what I was going to do. Both respected the old ways and must have known I wasn't made for a life in this town: marrying a shopkeeper or a farmer and raising a family. I was the kind of child who loved the old ways, listened to grandparents tell stories their grandparents had told them about the wonders in the days before the coming of the King Beneath the Hill. The King's magic was very strong, and he could read a thousand minds at once.

Witches were part of those days. The King crushed Sphinx and Sybil, Giant and Water God. But most witches, though some were caught and burned, evaded destruction through cunning and luck, lived quietly, and were ignored by the authorities.

But though Fey don't die, they do fade away eventually. So it was said to be with the King Beneath the Hill. He reigned but did not rule. His palace and the wondrous city of Maxee where he lived were far away. The Crown Prince was gone, and the other sons were known to be quarreling about the succession and too busy to care about us.

People went to Bertrade when they were sick or in trouble. If anyone ruled the town, it was the Witch. If she wished to see me, my parents would not refuse. So the next evening, wearing a wool sweater as well as my shift, I went alone down the path to the Oak of Avalon. The Witch sat alone on the porch, and there was tea and cake.

Before she started, she said, "I've never told this version of the story. I only heard it once and that was from my mother who was Witch of Avalon before me.

"Seven Frowns and Seven Smiles," she said—and paused—then began.

"Not many years after the invaders entered this land, Prince Alaric, the son of the King Who Rules, rode into the Forest of Avalon as though it was his. He was handsome and well liked among his kind and thought very well of himself.

"His parents had invited every princess, each lovelier than the next, to balls and fêtes. But Alaric was satisfied with none of them, because even the best was not good enough.

7

"Though he found himself alone and deep in a woods, Alaric had no fear. For the Fairy Lords and Ladies had given him at birth all manner of presents."

Again they all got listed: Bellephron the winged horse, the cape, the ring, the sword, the belt and britches, the boots. As before the list ended with: "But the crown from the King Who Rules was the greatest gift of all. For that permitted him to see the minds of others.

"On this bright morning a beautiful maiden watched the Prince's passage. But he couldn't see her for she was dressed in robes of green spider silk and blended right into the trees. She carried a long twisted gray stick.

"When she stepped onto the path and looked Alaric right in the eye, it was more an ambush than an encounter."

I listened to the story, felt it blend into the sounds of birds chirping at twilight, leaves whispering, something moving in the grass.

"Alaric smiled for the maiden the smile that won the heart of each and every princess. But this was Gerathea, Daughter of the Witch Queen, and she had heard of Alaric.

"Gerathea answered his smile with a frown and threw the curse given her by the Nixie of the Silver Pond who had lost her underwater home to the invaders.

"Alaric was startled when the horse disappeared from under him before he could fly away. But he landed on his feet and smiled again. Gerathea frowned and hurled the curse of the Dryad of the Farthest Moors whose lands had been taken by the Fey King.

"Alaric's robe disappeared before he could make himself invisible. The mourning chant of the Troll King took his ring before he noticed. His smile was hard as he reached for his sword. Her frown and the curse of the Gryphon of The Tall Mountain, uttered as he fell to his death, took sword and scabbard.

"Alaric's smile faltered as he moved towards Gerathea. But a frown and the dying prophecy of the Sybil of the Iron Throne took his boots before he could reach her. The last prayer of the Harvest Queen deprived him of belt and britches.

"On his head was the crown given him by his father the King Who Rules. Before he could go into Gerathea's mind, she uttered a spell of her own creation. She stepped forward with the twisted gray stick that was the wand given to her by her mother the Queen of Witches.

"Before he could go into her mind, she uttered a curse of her own making and knocked the crown from his head.

"Alaric stood helpless with nothing but a shirt to his name like the poorest of the poor.

"She struck him on his chest. The shirt fell away and he shrank back into a child, crying and trying to cover himself. Gerathea took his hand and led him deep into the woods. There he remains to this day."

I liked this version much better than the last. And there was the surprise, in fact a shock, at the end. It was said The King Beneath the Hill's own son, the crown prince, had been lost many years ago, and never found.

Bertrade looked at my face and knew all I was thinking. She smiled, which I'd not seen her do.

"Would you like to learn more?"

"Will I be able to do things like Gerathea?"

"Unlikely I'm afraid!" She smiled again. "It will be hard; harder than school. And you will live here." As she spoke an owl flew down and landed on her shoulder. "Minerva, my night companion," she said.

"My mother and father..."

"We will talk to them tonight." She rose and held out her hand. The owl watched as I grasped it. But then she looked away as if she was already used to me.

## 3.

That night and the revelations that followed are with me whenever there is a girl or even a boy who doesn't stop coming to my tellings when all others their age do. I haven't married and have no children. But the apprentices when they appear every few years are a substitute.

Nevya the current one is almost ready to go on her own to a town deep in the heart of the Forest. Though I've inherited the title of Witch of Avalon, there are quite a few of us in these woods. Almost every town and large village throughout the kingdom has one. We have spent our time well.

Now it's a boy, Diccon, age twelve who comes to hear me tell the tales. He's hounded by the other children. His father calls him worthless. If Diccon wishes, I will take him as an apprentice though it breaks tradition. In the coming crisis a boy may prove very useful.

I've been Witch of Avalon since Bertrade departed. Before she grew weary of this life, she transformed herself into an owl and flew away one night at harvest time. She and her familiar, Minerva, seemed to sail directly into the huge moon that filled the sky and disappear.

In memory our childhoods are times of wonder and the present is poor and mean. Truly, though my childhood was far better.

Now people are robbed on the roads. Now men are hanged for poaching on what was always public land, and farms are seized for taxes on a whim. My brother is mayor of my home town. People, especially the young, are angry and want to fight. He grows old with worry.

Fey eventually pass into a twilight world. The King Beneath the Hill by all reports is more in that world than not. And there is no clear Heir since the Crown Prince disappeared centuries ago. The struggle for succession among the brother princes entails great expense. The payment comes from the people.

In these last weeks of summer I told the story of the Smiles and Frowns as the Fey once told it. And I promised to tell it the next week as the Witches now tell it. For that telling, adults, mainly women, came and stood behind their children. They snickered at the plight of Alaric, applauded Gerathea, went home, and as I thought they would, talked about what they'd heard.

I promised then that tonight I would tell the story as people will tell it in years to come. The word has spread. This time many men young and old stand with the women. A tale should not only entertain but teach. Learning this one did that for me. Nevya sits with Diccon. I've talked to his father, and the boy will now stay with me. The crowd arranges itself around the porch, and I begin:

## Seven Wrongs and Seven Princes

Once there was a King Who Ruled and had great power and had seven sons. He loved them all and gave each a gift. To one a winged horse, to another a cloak of invisibility, to the third a ring that let him pass through walls, to the fourth a sword that could smash any weapon, to the fifth boots that carried one a thousand leagues, to the sixth a belt and britches of power that made him stronger than a hundred men. But he loved the eldest, Prince Alaric, the most and gave him a crown with which he could see into others' minds.

When one day the prince disappeared while hunting, the king searched for him for a year and a day, knew no happiness when he couldn't be found, and lost all interest in ruling. The brothers guessed and even hoped Alaric would never return. Each thought he would be king, and they fought with each other and plotted against each other.

The country fell into ruin. Neighboring kings invaded and burned villages and towns, bandits ruled the roads, pirates raided the fishing fleets, farmers couldn't plant their crops, thieves made off with the cattle and sheep. And still the king mourned and the brothers fought.

Then one day a solitary figure, a man in the robes of a traveling scholar, rode toward the castle on an old and tired horse. On his head he wore a crown. His brothers saw the figure from the castle walls and guessed who he was.

The brother who had been given a flying horse leapt on its back and flew at the traveler. As he swooped in the other man smiled a tired sad smile and put into his brother's mind the anger and despair of woodcutters whose forest had been burned. The flying horse disappeared, and the brother fell bottom first into a puddle.

Children in the audience clap their hands. Their parents nod approval.

The traveler continued on and the next brother wrapped himself in the cloak of invisibility. He was shown peddlers robbed and murdered on the royal highway. His cape disappeared, and he was too much a coward to act openly.

The brother with the ring saw miners trapped underground and smashed his face into a wall he tried to walk through. The brother with the sword found himself empty-handed when fishing boats smashing on the rocks appeared in his head.

The one with the magic boots saw unpaid soldiers starving and ended up barefoot. Then the one with belt and britches saw farmers with burned crops and found himself bare-assed.

The audience enjoys this, laughing and applauding.

Finally the eldest son, Prince Alaric, for it was he, entered the castle, climbed the stairs, and discovered his father alone in the throne room. The old man looked up amazed and rose, asking his son where he had been and what had happened to him. His crown still enabled him to see into others' minds.

He saw how his son had decided to lose his princely raiment and go through the kingdom finding out how the people lived and what they thought. When the father saw the near ruin to which the land was reduced, he wept and begged the son to take his crown and rule the country.

Then all his brothers swore allegiance. Alaric married a wise and beautiful woman he had met in his travels, ruled justly and well. The kingdom recovered and became prosperous once again.

People thank me for the tale. I tell them it isn't mine but was given to me in bits and pieces by visiting witches. Tales like this one, I tell them, are not truth or prophecy. They are made up of our fears and hopes. Witches have told this story in many places.

I don't tell them the stories about Prince Alaric, which we Witches share with no one else. Nevya accompanies the visitors back to town and answers questions about what they've just heard.

## 4.

Only Diccon and I remain. I put my hand on his shoulder and lead him to where Reynard my familiar sits in the shadows. The fox allows himself to be patted, which says much in the boy's favor. No one would suspect a male of being a Witch, and Diccon is eager to learn.

So I bring him to the other side of the Oak to a small locked hut and tell him what he's about to see. Diccon is wide-eyed. I open the door, cause light to shine, and show him what Bertrade showed me on my first night in Avalon. A pale figure, a man in a shirt, Prince Alaric under heavy enchantment stares wide-eyed at Diccon, who stares back.

The Prince was ambushed in this forest long before I or Bertrade or her mother was born. For the generations since he was captured we Sisters have passed him around, taking him to parts of his kingdom he would never have visited, showing him subjects he would never have seen otherwise. I always try to make sure he's here in Avalon when a new apprentice comes to me.

Originally he was kept on the move to prevent his being recaptured. I doubt if anyone is looking for him now. These days, his return would be a thunderbolt that would upset far too many of his brothers' plans.

He always begs to be free, says he's learned about the sorrows and hardships in the land. He promises to rule wisely. The question is whether he can be trusted, and we all have our doubts. Our attempts to Foretell have yielded no clear vision of the future. "Seven Wrongs and Seven Princes" is a hope, not a prediction.

We can never be sure, and yet we must act soon or never. As this happens I will instruct young Diccon in our arts and hope this world holds a place for him and all of us. I doubt if I will but perhaps he will live to see a further turning of the tale that began long before the Smiles and Frowns.

Illustration by Arthur Rackham for *Gulliver's Travels* by
Jonathan Swift, 1909

# The Cinnamon Cavalier

One fine May afternoon the Royal cook popped the Cavalier out of the baking ovens of the Giant King's castle. Since he was intended from the first for the King's only daughter and only child, no effort had been spared. The heat of the kitchen shimmered in the sunlight as he was brought forth.

It is a truism that few who serve giants are themselves gigantic. For instance, the head pastry cook who officiated was a large man as such things run, though you've doubtless seen them taller and even some greater around.

Under his direction, pantry boys, scullion lads, and baker's assistants hauled a dairy's worth of butter, sacks of flour and sugar to a huge tub and poured it all in. The cook himself produced a small teak chest from far Ceylon and into the mix tossed the spice that hints at excitement, danger, and arousal: cinnamon. He then supervised the crew as they used oars to whip the ingredients into a smooth batter.

A mold the size and shape of a mortal man was brought in and placed on a pan big enough to hold the cook himself. The batter was poured with all the usual fuss associated with baking a cookie as large as many of us. Hair curled in the heat as the oven door was opened, and with a heave and ho the pan was placed inside.

After time had passed, the oven was opened again and the fires banked. After all had cooled enough, frosting was applied: chocolate for the hair and boots, berry blue for the pants, strawberry for the vest, which was buttoned with apricots. His eyes were almonds and his nose walnuts. He had a shining vanilla smile that matched the sword he held in his right hand, while in his left he grasped a single rose as red as cherries, a champion and suitor created out of pastry.

Only when the work was finished did the eyes blink and the sword arm move.

Those who saw first thought it was the oven's heat, the long hours, the cooking brandy. Only when he sat up did a long gasp emerge from the kitchen staff. "See here!" said the pastry chef.

Mainly it's engineering that's involved in providing for the comforts of a fifty-foot-tall man and his family. But there is magic around a giant's castle. The tap of a divine finger on the cook's soul might have been what brought life to the pastry, or perhaps it was a stray spell picked up in some spice caravan or sailing ship en route to the kitchen.

Who is to say what produces a hero? From what little we know, heroism is instinctive. Hercules strangled serpents while still in his cradle; as a boy Arthur unthinkingly drew forth Excalibur.

So it was this time when the Cinnamon Cavalier swung his legs off the platter and hopped to the floor. Everyone else in the kitchen fell back toward the wide swinging doors. "Get back up there," said the chef indignantly. The almond eyes turned his way. The sword twitched.

Cooks are well known to be full of bluster but deep cowards. And this one was no exception. When the hero took one stiff step his way, the chef broke and led a panicked mob through the big double doors.

Off they ran, yelling about horror and cookies. The hero was about to follow them, when he saw a lifeboat set on wheels and full of steaming soup, an ox cart only just large enough for the chicken pie it held. He saw an empty wagon right inside the door, the place in the giant's daughter's supper train that would have been his.

A hero is unlike us in enough ways to show us we are human. Turning away from ordinary fate, he saw a small iron door at the other side of the kitchen and went to it. With scarcely a moment's fumbling, he pushed the bar aside and set out on his adventures. With each action, his movement became more fluid, his sword gleamed like polished metal, dew formed on the rose. Through all that happened, though, he never lost a certain stiffness. He was, after all, a cookie.

The Cavalier found himself in a passage lighted by torches and with two flights of stairs. One led down, the other up. The way down smelled rank, the way up fresh. As he paused before the stairs, chains rattled and two gleaming eyes rushed up toward him.

Just as most servants of a giant are human sized, some few are not. Ratmagnus, the guardian of the lower ways, was six feet long from the tip of his tail to the nose, which twitched at the scent of approaching food. Up the stairs he came, dragging the chain on his studded metal collar. Ravening with hunger, Ratmagnus, all sharp teeth and matted fur, leaped the last five steps. It's claws raked the hero's chest in a shower of crumbs.

The sword passed into his mouth and down his throat. One twist of the hero's wrist, and the rodent gurgled, twitched along his whole length, and fell back into the dark. It was only then that the hero felt his destiny and turned upward on the stairs. From behind him in the kitchen came the tramp of feet, the clank of arms. The yells of the kitchen staff had brought the castle guard.

Up forty steps the Cinnamon Cavalier bounded. A massive door lay before him. He shoved against it, but it was locked. He rapped the lock with his sword, but it held. Below, soldiers shouted about the corpse of Ratmagnus and began a quick march up the stairs.

The cavalier brushed the lock with the hand that held the rose, and the door sprang open. He rushed through, slammed it behind him, and stood on the walkway atop the curtain wall of the Giant's castle.

The walkway ran as far as the eye could see. He looked one way and saw below him the roaring river that formed the moat. He looked the other, and the castle keep loomed against a background of hulking mountains and ancient sequoias.

Black turrets and silver towers crenulated and encrusted with gargoyles caught the light of a glorious afternoon. And there he found the true destiny that every hero, flesh or dough, instantly recognizes.

At one of the hundred windows was a face, round and curious, watching him with fascination. The Giant's daughter was a jolly child with legs wide as tree stumps and feet like boulders. She skipped rope and chimneys fell down miles away. But in such a setting and seen with almond eyes, her face was perfection. The attraction of children to cookies is well known. But the opposite is also true.

The giant child's nursemaid, a behemoth who had also tended her mother, was twelve feet tall and only came to her young charge's waist. Her tutor was a captive scholar, a thin man with a nasal voice who sat chained to the edge of a shelf and called out his lessons to his enormous pupil.

Once her father's counselors said, "Oh, your immenseness, the princess has kicked over another barn."

The Giant King, amused and proud in the way of fathers, thundered, "Damn it, give her dancing lessons." And twice a week, a tiny ballet mistress tried to teach her to be a snowflake.

The Cinnamon Cavalier saw the giant princess's eyes widen at the same moment that he heard the door fly open behind him. Soldiers, armed and helmeted, poured onto the parapet. They halted and waited as heavy footsteps sounded behind them. The guards stepped back and Goliath, as they called him, heaved into view.

Even in the Land of the Giants, as we've said, few are actually gigantic. But giants like everyone else have moments when their passions stray. Some such indiscretion had produced the soldier who lumbered through the door.

Goliath stood well over ten feet tall. His size and the iron club he swung had always been enough. Enemies ran before him at first sight. This time he paused and stared, amazed. For a cookie barely cool from the oven, however, Goliath was no more a wonder than everything else.

21

With one backward glance to the face in the tower window, the Cinnamon hero went to meet his challenger. A short affray it was. The club swung where the cookie had been. The white sword flicked. With one stiff little skip the cookie jumped aside as Goliath fell, howling about the cut on his knee.

The Cinnamon Man, legs opening and closing like scissors, ran along the parapet heading toward the castle keep and the face at the window. The guards at first fell back before him.

But their captain, too, was aware of the towers and their windows. He knew that at any moment they might be seen by one of the of Giant's ministers. Or even, terrible thought, by the King himself. The captain ordered the men to form a wall with their shields. He ordered up the Royal Archers. The Cinnamon Cavalier ran forward, waving his white sword, almond eyes flashing.

The shield line began to waver. And then the first arrows flew. One flicked away a piece of the candied lemon rind that was his left ear. Behind him more archers took up position and opened fire. One snipped a small chip off his right elbow. The guards cheered and began to edge forward.

"We'll reduce that foolish cookie to a pile of crumbs," bellowed the captain.

"The dessert, ruined, ruined," wailed the pastry chef. "Quick, prepare a hasty pudding."

The Cinnamon Man ran at them, and they fell back. But more arrows flew and more crumbs scattered in the spring breeze. As the two lines of guards closed in, he jumped onto the outer wall. Below him raced a river in full flood. He knew, by instinct, that he would not last long in water. Before the plunge, he gazed up at the window. The Giant King's daughter was not looking his way. Her hand was extended as though she had just flung something, and she gazed upward.

A black shadow fell on the parapet. The archers flinched and ducked their heads. The Cavalier heard a harsh shriek and looked up in time to see the great beak and the fierce talons that hooked onto his back and pulled him up into the sky. Every man on the castle walls bowed down in fear and respect.

The Cinnamon Cavalier soared toward the tower and through a window large enough for a schooner to sail into under full sail. The eager, curious child presented her left wrist, on which the Roc landed. Before she returned her pet to its cage, she released the cookie from its talons' grasp.

Standing on the huge table on which she placed him, the Cavalier knelt and presented to her the cherry red rose. Delighted as the large can be at the tiny and exquisite, she held it on the tip of a finger, smiled and said, "We thank you Sir Cavalier," in a voice not yet quite like thunder.

The Giant's Daughter was a young lady who ate a barge of fish for Friday dinner and puddings wide as ponds. Now you might think that a child, as greedy as you were at ten and huge in ways only a ten-year-old can imagine, would have seized the cookie and gobbled him up.

But she was a bright and imaginative soul who had watched his progress on the walls and through the air. And he smiled his bright frosting smile as if that possibility had never occurred to him.

She put him on a shelf along with such keepsakes as the Sphinx who sat and asked his silly riddle each time she tickled his belly and the Phoenix, with which she was supposed to play only in Nurse's presence, which consumed itself just before bedtime and grew whole again by noonday.

The Roc scrabbled in his cage, and the Giant Princess went back to her lessons. She looked at the Cinnamon Cavalier, and you might wonder how long it would be even with the best will in the world before she became bored and hungry as inevitably she must.

Perhaps she will find a quest for him, send him forth again on the path of the hero. She will promise herself to offer him his freedom if he succeeds, but when he does, she will break the promise.

Whichever way it falls out, be assured that his fate will be great and memorable. Quite unlike what probably lies in store for you and me.

Illustration by Arthur Rackham for *Undine* by Friedrich de la Motte Fouque, 1909

# The Margay's Children

## 1.

Not to boast, but I'd say I'm pretty good as a godfather. As an actual parent, I'd doubtless have been a disaster. But I have six godchildren, and I love all of them. Selesta is the second eldest and my secret favorite. When she was real small, three and four years old, I had Mondays off, and her mother, my friend Joan Mata, would leave her with me while she kept doctors' appointments and met her design clients in the city.

That was when Selesta and I first talked about cats. At the time, I had an apartment on Second Avenue in the teens, and on the ground floor of the building facing mine was a row of small shops, each of which had a cat. Selesta took a great interest in them. That could just have been because she couldn't have a cat of her own.

The Italian deli had a majestic tricolor cat named Maybelline. As a deli cat she had plenty of food, numerous admirers whom she would allow to pet her as she sat in the sun by the front door, and mice to keep her busy at night.

The Russian cobbler next door had a thin gray cat with a truncated tail that twitched back and forth. A shoe repair shop has no food and probably few mice. The cobbler was thin and gray himself, and when I once asked him the cat's name, he just shook his head like he'd never heard of such a thing. So I decided to call him Hank, and Selesta agreed with me.

The third store was a Vietnamese nail and hair and massage shop with elaborate neon signage. It employed a trio of ladies with elaborate nails and one very silly man. Their cat was a Siamese named Mimi or something like that. Mimi had a wardrobe of exotic sweaters and collars and even booties.

She was usually carried by one of the ladies. When she passed by, the other cats' noses and ears twitched as if they could sense a cat nearby but couldn't tell where it was.

To amuse ourselves, Selesta and I made up stories about the three cats and their adventures. Once they all went out to find a pair of red striped socks for Hank on his birthday. Another time they went to the moon, which was run by a bunch of gangster mice.

Maybe there I should have discouraged her interest. However, I believe Joan had asked me to be the godfather of her only child because we went back so far and shared so many secrets.

Eventually Selesta's parents moved to Hoboken, she started school, and our Monday afternoons and the adventures of the store cats were no more.

It was a few years later when she was eight or nine that Selesta first asked me questions about Joan and the situation that had made us friends. It was the Wednesday after her birthday, and I'd just taken her to see a matinee performance of *Cats* on Broadway. That had been her wish, and her mother had no objection.

The kick in taking a kid to the theater is seeing and sharing their unbridled wonder. Afterwards we discussed the show and let the crowd carry us to the subway. I noticed that Selesta now had her mother's green eyes flecked with gold.

"My favorite part was the end where the cat goes up to heaven," she said.

"On the old rubber tire," I replied. "That's the way it always happens with cats."

"My mother says she has allergies, so I can't have a cat or dog."

This sudden swerve in our conversation took me by surprise. "She *is* allergic, honey," I said automatically— and immediately regretted it. Kids are uncanny. Selesta knew I had lied, just as she suspected that her mother was lying.

She followed it up by saying, "Once when I was little you told me you and mommy lived in a house with a mystery cat. Like Macavity in the play."

Macavity, the villain of the musical, seemed to me too over the top to be very scary. The animal Selesta referred to had been very quiet and quite real.

"That was long before you were born or even thought of," I said as the matinee crowds carried us down the subway stairs.

It bothered me that I had no recollection of ever having told her about the cat or about Anise's Place on East Tenth Street. That was the semi-crash pad where Joan

Mata and I first met, back in those legendary times, the late '60s.

"What was the cat's name?"

By then we were waiting amid a crowd of commuters at 33rd Street for the PATH train to Hoboken. I began the story, and as I did, she listened with exactly the same rapt expression she'd had at the show.

"He was called Trebizon. That was an ancient city far away on the Black Sea. Anise, his owner, was a lady who had started to get a doctorate in history before she became a hippy and decided to let a bunch of people come live with her."

"You and my mother were hippies!" The idea amused her.

"I guess I was. You'd have to ask your mother if she was." Back then, my foothold in the city had been fragile. A stupid romantic quarrel, the kind a young man has at twenty-one, had put me out of the place where I'd been living and sent me crashing at Anise's. But I didn't go into that.

"What was Trebizon like?"

"He was a big old orange cat who seemed very smart." I didn't tell her that the people living in that neighborhood and in that apartment had achieved a really rarified degree of psychic awareness and mind expansion. Apparently Trebizon shared this.

"It seemed he always had a favorite. When I first came to stay there, he spent every night on the chest of a very quiet stranger, a kid from the South who slept on the living room couch. Anise joked that the cat had adopted him.

"All of a sudden, every time a newcomer entered the apartment, the cat would get off his chest and sit and watch. The kid would take off all his clothes, kneel down on the floor in front of the new arrival, and kiss his or her feet."

"He kissed your feet?" she was fascinated.

"It was creepy and embarrassing. But I noticed other people were pleased when it happened. Like they said to themselves, *Finally people are kissing my feet!* I also saw that Trebizon acted like an owner whose pet had done a clever trick.

"I guess word got back to the kid's family. Because one day his parents appeared and took him home."

"What did Trebizon do?"

"Found someone else who lived there, a dreamy kind of girl who was studying to be a dancer. The cat slept beside her in this bed in a little alcove near the kitchen. We called her the Flower Girl because she brought home the single roses that gypsy ladies sold in bars and little sprays of lilies of valley, potted geraniums.

"Then it escalated. She began coming in with bridal bouquets, with boxes of red carnations, huge bunches of violets. The crash pad began to look like a funeral parlor. Trebizon prowled among them, chewed the ferns, and batted the petals that fell to the floor.

"The Flower Girl started to look furtive, haunted. One time she came home with two shopping bags full of yellow daffodils. Another time it was orchids. Stuff she'd probably stolen. She'd put them on the floor around her bed, and Trebizon would lie there like it was his altar.

"Eventually the police nabbed her as she was ripping off a bank of tulips from the Macy's garden show. With her gone, Trebizon began to notice me."

The train arrived right then, and we didn't get seats. I held onto a pole and Selesta held onto me. We sang scraps of the songs. She knew a lot of the lyrics. The other passengers pretended we weren't there.

I hoped my god daughter would forget what we'd been talking about. Telling the story had reminded me of what it was like to be young and confused and with no place to hide when a demon closes in.

But as soon as we hit the platform of Hoboken terminal Selesta asked, "Where was my mother when the cat came after you?"

Hoboken twenty years ago was still such a compact old-fashioned working-class city that in my memory it's all black and white like an old newsreel. We walked from the station to Newark Street where a sign in the shape of a giant hand pointed its finger at the Clam Broth House. On the way, I told Selesta, "Right when the cat began to stalk me was when your mother appeared. Trebizon sat in the doorway of the room where I slept and stared at me. I had no other place to go, and I sat on my bed wondering what I was going to do.

"Then I looked up, and there was this girl a little older than me, wearing the shortest miniskirt in the world. She put her bags in the alcove where the Flower Girl had stayed. Her name was Joan Mata. She looked taller than she was, and she had amazing eyes—green and gold like yours. Your mother had been in Europe for the summer. She and Anise had met at Columbia, and she knew Trebizon from back then.

"I didn't even have to tell her what was happening. She gave one look at Trebizon, and he ran and hid in the kitchen."

What Joan had actually done was let out a low growl. Trebizon's reaction was like that of the cobbler's cat and the deli cat when Mimi was carried past. His nose and ears twitched; he looked around, scared and confused like he sensed a cat but couldn't see one.

Trebizon never came back out of that kitchen. Anise knew something was wrong, but she and the cat were both a bit afraid of Joan.

"Why didn't Trebizon make my mother allergic," Selesta asked suddenly.

Before I could think of a reply, a voice said, "The allergies developed later, honey." Joan Mata stood smiling at the front entrance of the sprawling block-long maze of dining rooms that was the Clam Broth House.

Joan was a designer. She was married to Selesta's father, the architect Frank Gallen. He was out of town. Their townhouse was like a showcase for his work and hers. Some part of it was always being rebuilt or redesigned. That week it was the kitchen.

So we ate at the restaurant, which Selesta always loved. The three of us were seated. When Joan put on her glasses to glance at a menu, they always seemed to alight on her face for a moment. Like a butterfly.

Selesta recounted scenes from the musical and chunks of our conversation. "And he said he was a hippy but he didn't know if you were."

"Your godfather has it backwards," said Joan. "Everything I owned was in those suitcases. He had a job. It was so cute, every morning in that madhouse, he'd put on his suit and tie and go off to write fashion copy."

Selesta asked, "What happened to Trebizon?"

Neither of us knew. "I imagine he had a few lives left." Joan said.

Selesta left us briefly, reluctantly, for the ladies room, knowing that in her absence secrets would be discussed.

"She asked and I told her a little bit about Trebizon and East Tenth Street."

"That's perfect. She's getting curious, and I'm glad it happened like this and with you."

"Shouldn't you tell her about your father?"

She sighed. "She'll ask, and I'll tell her."

Over twenty years before, we had known we'd be friends from the moment we met. In late night conversations on the front steps and back fire escape on East Tenth Street, we talked about sex and drugs and parents and trauma.

Joan sat on railings and never lost her balance. She was only a year or two older than I was but knew so much more. Her mother was a well-known lawyer, her father was Antonio Mata, the Mexican painter who did surrealistic paintings that looked like cartoons and signed himself, "Margay."

That night, for the first time I questioned her judgment but said nothing.

## 2.

About ten years later when Selesta was in her late teens, a sophomore studying theater at NYU, there was a Friday afternoon when she drove us both out to Long

Island. We were going to spend the weekend with her mother and grandmother in The House That Ate The World. It was early June, and the Island was radiant.

That uncanny light you get on that thin, low strip of land on a long afternoon is sunlight reflected off the Atlantic and Long Island Sound.

Selesta was slim but not as painfully thin as she had been a few years before when her parents divorced and she became bulimic. She had been cured of that, and in high school had lived a tightly scheduled life, the point of which, maybe, was to prevent her pondering too much about who she was.

A couple of times over the years, though, we'd talked about her mother and our adventures when we first met. I'd run through my stories of Joan and me dancing at Ondine with Hendrix in the house and talking to Alan Ginsberg in Tompkins Park. All the baggage of the tiresomely hip older generation got trotted out.

That day, though, she asked, "You know about ocelots?" I nodded; I had a good idea where the conversation was going.

"They're small; their bodies are a couple of feet long and with a tail almost that long. They have beautiful coats," she said. "They live all through South America and Mexico. Whenever I go anywhere, if they have a zoo I check and see if they have ocelots. San Diego does and Cincinnati.

"Ocelots are shy," she said. "And, of course, they're getting scarce because of their fur and the forest disappearing.

"Obviously, though, what I'm really interested in is the Margay, a kind of cousin with the same markings. You know about them."

"They live and hunt in trees," I said. "They're nocturnal, very, very shy and getting rare."

"You know that because my mother talked to you about this, didn't she? Back when you were kids. She knew about all this, about her father. You know Margay was his nickname? I first got interested in them when I was about twelve and heard about Grandfather Margay from Grandma Ruth.

"Ruth took me to Mexico last summer. We went to the town where Antonio Mata was born and grew up. There were still people who knew him. We made a special visit to Belize because of this amazing zoo they have. It's away from the coast with lots of space. More like a nature park with all animals from Central America," she said.

"I waited outside the Margay enclosure, and at dusk I saw one on a high tree branch. Its eyes reflected the light. Other people were there, but it looked at me. Then it was gone."

As we rolled along the flat prairie that is the Island's center, late afternoon sunlight made long shadows and gave a kind of magic to the endless strip malls, the buildings with signboards listing dermatologists' and dentists' offices, the used car lots.

Selesta said, seemingly out of nowhere, "Trebizon may have been possessed, but the way he acted with my mother is how a domestic cat reacts to a wild one."

I realized that Joan must never have talked to her about any of this. "You're right, honey," I said. "That's what it was like."

Keeping her eyes on the road, she reached over with her left hand and pulled down the shoulder of her blouse. There was a small patch of tawny fur with a touch of black.

"How long have you had that?"

"A few years. It was just a speck and then it grew. I knew what it was when it appeared. I shaved it at first and was afraid someone would find out. Lately I've let it grow."

I watched her staring at the road, tried to see a cat shape in her head. She glanced my way, and for a moment her eyes did catch the light.

"Your mother had the same thing when I first knew her. She had to get rid of it with electrolysis. Painful stuff."

"My mother never volunteers information about things like this. When I first got this I asked her what it meant. She mentioned her father very briefly then told me about laser treatment."

"But you didn't want that."

"I want to remember. Maybe understand something."

We drove in silence for a while. Then Selesta said, "She was only a few years older than I am now when you met. How much did she know?"

"She had just figured out what had happened to her and to her brother Luis. She was mad that your grandmother hadn't been able to tell her more. But I think Ruth must have been in shock herself back then. I think your mother was too. Maybe that's what made them so dedicated to their work."

"Look in that portfolio," she said and indicated one stuck in between our seats.

It contained photos. The first few were of her grand-father, Antonio Mata. As a young man he was thin and poised. Maybe his head and face seemed a bit stream-lined. But I might have been seeing that because of what I knew. He was with a group of young people in one picture at a country house in Mexico. I recognized Frida Kahlo in the crowd. In another picture, Antonio Mata in his shirt sleeves painted on a canvas.

I had seen these before. Joan had shown them to me when I first knew her. There was one of Antonio Mata and Ruth, Joan's mother, which I remembered having seen. They made a handsome couple. Ruth wore shorts and a man's shirt.

After her husband's disappearance Ruth went to Co-lumbia law school, married the civil rights lawyer Harry Rosen, and became a legal counsel for Amnesty Inter-national.

"Look at the next one," Selesta said.

This one was new to me. Antonio Mata lay stretched out on the branch of a tree looking at the camera with cat's eyes. "And the next."

The picture had probably been taken at dusk on a porch. A light was on inside the house. Mata was a bit older than in the other shots. He was poised with his hands on the rails as if he was going to leap into the gathering dark. He looked like he was trapped. I recog-nized the porch and the house.

"Your mother gave you these?"

"My grandmother. She took them."

The next picture was of three children standing on the front porch of the place that Mata called, "The House That Ate The World." They ranged in age from nine to maybe three. The oldest was a very serious boy who seemed to be looking at something in the distance. This, I knew was Joan's brother Luis. The youngest was Joan's sister, Catherina, smiling and holding something up to the camera with both hands. Joan was right in between. She gazed up at her brother.

"I'd never seen a picture of her brother."

"There aren't many. They say he was very shy around strangers. A true Margay. Just look at him! Those eyes!"

"He died very young."

"Eighteen," she said. "Drowned in the Great South Bay a few years after his father disappeared back into Mexico. Water killed the cat. Everyone knew it was suicide."

It's tough when a friend you love and respect is doing something you think may be dumb and wrong. "Your mother was still torn up about that and her father's disappearance when I first knew her," I said like I was pleading her case. "She really had no one to talk to."

Selesta drove in silence. The sun was going down. I looked at the pictures of the Mata paintings that she had in her portfolio. I found "The House That Ate The World."

It's the house in the old rural Hamptons in which Antonio Mata had lived for some years with his wife and children. In the painting it's distended, bulging. Through open windows and doors flow furniture and phonographs, tennis shoes and radios, refrigerators and easy chairs.

Out of the house and onto the lawn in front and the meadow in back they tumble: cocktail dresses and ice buckets, strollers and overcoats, the possessions of an American household circa 1948.

"Kind of quaint compared to what's inside an American house today," I said.

"I don't think it's about materialism so much as about wariness and curiosity," Selesta said. "And maybe fear. He's a feline in human territory."

"Are you afraid, honey? Like he was?"

"Sometimes I am. I think it's good to be a little afraid sometimes."

We drove for a while before she asked, "Was my mother ever afraid."

"Not that I saw when she was your age. She only seemed to get scared after you were born."

We talked a little more about her family. Brief bursts of conversation took place amid stretches of silence.

It was dark when we parked at the entrance to the driveway of The House That Ate The World. Lamps were on inside, but Joan stood on the unlighted porch and smiled as we approached.

"She can see us in the dark," muttered Selesta. "She just shrugs when I ask her about it."

We all embraced and Joan asked, "How was traffic?"

"No problem," said her daughter, stepping past her. "How are you?"

By night, it could almost still be the cottage of fifty years before. I caught the tang and murmur of the ocean. A few hundred yards away the tide was coming in.

Through the open windows I saw the easel in the living room with the half-finished painting. Bulbous circa 1950 American cars bore down on the viewer. Antonio Mata had disappeared without finishing it.

"A cat's eye view of the highway," I murmured.

Joan looked at me and then at her daughter, who smiled. Neither said anything, but they moved down the hall to the kitchen, not touching but walking together.

When they were alone, Joan would ask her daughter what she and I had talked about on the way out here. I was glad to have given them that opening.

"Hello Richie," said a familiar voice behind me. I turned, and standing at the back porch door was the woman from the 1950s snapshots. Then Ruth Mata Rosen moved and that illusion disappeared. Decades obviously had passed, and now she walked with a cane.

Ruth had called me Richie the first time we met many years before. There was no reason for it that I've ever been able to discover. Nobody else in the world has ever used that nickname for me.

"They're alone together?" she asked.

"In the kitchen," I said.

"No yelling? No screams?" she asked. "I don't neces-sarily hear. Especially things I don't want to hear."

"Quiet so far."

"At first, with my background in negotiation, I tried to arbitrate their dispute," said Ruth. "What I discovered was that when you've spent nine years married to the cat man and never asked some basic questions, you're not dealing from a position of moral authority or common sense."

"We've all done things like that."

"Truly, have you ever done anything quite like that?"

"Well…"

"No. I was naïve and bedazzled and just plain stupid. And a lot of misfortune came from that."

"You did something fine with Selesta."

41

"I'd been back to the place where Antonio was born a couple of times. There are still people who remember him as a kid. A few of the locals had folk tales about tree cats who can take human form. Rumors run that his grandmother was one."

"Poor Joan," Ruth said. "When she was Selesta's age and wanted so much to find out about her father, there was a travel ban in that area. It was a dangerous place. The government was killing student dissidents. And right then I was busy."

The kitchen door opened. Selesta emerged and then Joan. A kind of truce seemed to have been arranged.

"Is anyone else hungry?" asked Ruth.

"Yes," said Joan. "But the sad thing is, none of us can cook."

Selesta narrowed her eyes and flashed her teeth. "I can probably rustle up something fresh and tasty from outside."

Joan winced, but I chuckled. Ruth said, "Suit yourself. However there are take-out menus on the refrigerator door. I thought maybe Thai would be nice."

### 3.

In the way of the busy lives we lead, it was a few years before I found myself back at The House That Ate The World. This time I drove out there with Joan and again arrived after dark. It was the middle of the week and a bit before Memorial Day. The neighbors weren't yet in residence; the Season and the Hampton traffic jams hadn't begun.

Again by night, with a sea breeze and little sound beside the slow rhythm of the Atlantic, the house could well have been the one in the Mata paintings, the old snapshots of the family.

Adding to that illusion, there were children in the cottage. Joan's younger sister Catherina was taking care of her granddaughters aged three and four and had brought them to see Great-grandmother Ruth.

The next morning, though, I stood on the porch with a mug of tea and 1950 was gone. The pond had been drained decades ago, and a summer mansion had been built on the site. A more recent and even larger vacation home now stood on the meadow. The House That Ate The World, by comparison, now seemed like a charming relic of the past.

Joan came out and sat on the porch swing. Two years before she'd had a brush with cancer. We all held our breaths, but it seemed to have been removed in time and that she was free and clear. Joan and I had become close again in ways we hadn't been since we were kids back on East Tenth Street.

She talked on her cell phone with her business partner about a corporate logo they were designing. Then she got a call from Selesta, who was driving out to the Hamptons with her husband Sam.

They'd gotten married a couple of years before. Sammy was a nice young man with a shaved head. Selesta had a tattoo on her throat that matched the blue of his eyes.

Recently she'd told all of us that she was pregnant and that she and Sam had decided to have the child. That news was always in the background now. Her mother and grandmother discussed obstetricians and hospitals. Selesta didn't understand why she might need a doctor who was discreet.

"Because you don't want to end up on the front page of the *National Enquirer*," Joan said. She shook her head when she got off the phone.

"Selesta told me once that it was good to always be a little scared," I told her.

"She won't know what fear is until she becomes a parent."

Two very busy young ladies returned with Catherina from the beach. Each carried a dripping pail. "We found living clams," they told us. Though the clams looked as dead as could be, we exclaimed over them.

Ruth sat out on the lawn under a large umbrella. Her great-grand-daughters went to show her the living clams.

"I married the least cat-like man in the world," Joan said. "I didn't really understand that was what I was doing. That was his main qualification. Then Selesta was born, and I saw it hadn't worked. I wasn't used to my plans going awry. Not even my unformulated ones."

"You told Selesta all this?"

"Recently I told her everything. Like you said."

"The vestigial tail?" Joan had to have one removed when she was child.

She nodded.

Later that afternoon I sat with Ruth and the little girls. "Richie, you'd think after I'd made such a mess out of my children's lives they wouldn't trust me with their offspring. But you'd be wrong. Someone always needs to dump their kids."

None of Catherina's three daughters had shown the slightest trace of the Margay. This was true also of her oldest daughter's two children.

"It's right out of Mendel," Ruth said. Poor Luis was at one end. Catherina's at the other. Joan is somewhere in between.

She was scratching her great-granddaughter's back. The child suddenly gave a big yawn and arched her back like a kitten.

Ruth looked at me with an expression that said, "You've got to wonder."

Later when Selesta and Sam showed up, I told them, "Selesta, much as I love you, you're grown up. You never want toys, you don't like musicals anymore. I mean, how do I justify going to lousy shows if I can't say I'm taking a kid? I want to be the godfather, maybe the god-grand-father to your kid."

"That's the main reason we decided to have a child," she said, and Sam nodded his agreement.

She looked out at Ruth on her lounge chair with the children around her and said, "I want that for Joan."

## Postscript

When you visit a maternity ward you scarcely know you're in a hospital. It's about life instead of illness, about bedazzled adults and the tiny, red-faced dictators who are going to run their lives.

Selesta's child was a boy, the first male born into the family since Luis Mata almost seventy years before.

I got to hold him. It's nice, but in truth I like kids better when they're standing up and talking. There's a wonderful stuffed ocelot that I'm planning to give him. It could as easily be a Margay. Selesta will be good with that.

Ruth was there in a motorized wheel chair with her care giver.

"A perfectly normal baby," said the very discreet doctor.

"Meaning he doesn't have a tail," said Joan quietly when the doctor left.

"Not yet, anyway," murmured Ruth.

Illustration by Arthur Rackham for *The Sleeping Beauty* by
C. S. Evans, 1920

# The Progress of Solstice and Chance

Never was there such a celebration as when the Queen of Summer wed the King of Winter. The Four Winds, mutual relatives of the bride and groom, in a fit of champagne-fueled excitement, blew open every door and window in the Palace of Time. Old Cronus himself, last and greatest of the First Gods, officiated in the high domed palace. Standing by to assist him if he faltered were the Lord of Life, smiling as always, and his wife, the blank-faced Lady of Death. But Cronus still remembered all the words and rituals.

The young cousins, all of them off-spring of the gods and descendants of Cronus, played at Flowers and Cups on the shaded pathways of the Arbor of Gossiping Trees. Chance, a tiny child with her mother Fate's wise gray eyes and father Folly's bright red hair, listened to the rustling leaves above her as those trees that could glimpse the ceremony described it to the ones further back.

"Is this," one tree whispered, "a marriage of love or convenience?"

"Both really," another tree replied. "The love affair of the King of Winter and Lady Death has been derailed by the Lord of Life. You know he engineered this marriage to thwart his wife." But at that moment one of Chance's cousins cried when a slightly older one swept up all his flowers in her cup, and Chance heard no more.

A year for the Gods is generations for mortals. The newly married couple spent half of each of their years in his kingdom and half in hers. Each autumn their Progress rolled through the days and months as they traveled from her palace in the tropics to his northern castle. Each spring they traveled back again. They enjoyed each other's company early on.

Before they got bored a daughter was born with her father's hair like frost and her mother's lovely bronze skin. Her name was Solstice, and at her presentation at the Palace of Time the godparents were Fate and Folly, she with her locked book, he in his costume of cap and bells.

Cronus was present but remained seated through the ceremony. Life and Death walked side by side down the Boulevard of Ecstasy and into the Palace to preside. As the godparents recited their pledges to look after the well-being of the child, Winter and Summer gave full attention to their infant daughter.

Those who studied Life and Death noticed that their eyes never met. His remained fixed on the ceiling. Hers wandered from Winter to Summer and back again.

From the doorway of the Ballroom of Forgotten Dances, young Chance watched with a bit of her mother Fate's dispassion and a touch of her father Folly's rueful smile. Behind her the cousins played the Game of Skulls and Crowns on the black and white marble floor. One of them crowed with laughter when he won for the black team by capping Mordred's skull with Charlemagne's crown. Invisible musicians played a lilting but piquant jig to which listeners would tap their feet and that no one could remember later.

＊

What Solstice liked best about her childhood was not the palm trees and blue waters of her mother's palace or her father's castle of ice and snow; it was the journey that started at the end of each summer and the Divine Progress through harvest time and into winter. The grand barges were draped with gold cloth and white silk; sails snapped as they crossed open water, and the oar masters' drums beat in rhythm as they plied up rivers. On the shore harvesters squinted against the sun to catch a glimpse of the Gods.

Her parents tended to ignore the people who came out to worship them. But when Solstice was held aloft, she would wave, and the crowds would sing her praises. Gods can be almost any size that suits them. At moments Winter and Summer and even Solstice could be giants. Harvest altars with mortal renderings of the child's smiling image and decorated with corn and pumpkins and game birds were erected along their way.

Grass turned from green to amber, leaves blazed with color. Her parents rode with hunting parties, and she followed on a pony amid an entourage of dwarf nursemaids and monkey servants.

The landscape turned gray and iron black; great flights of birds flew overhead; thin ice formed on standing water. Fires warmed the great tents as the Progress made its way to the outskirts of Winter.

Snow flew and horses pulled their sleds over firm river ice. Firelight flickered in log cabins. Parties of wood-cutters came out of the fir forests with great stacks of kindling gathered for the huge bonfires that marked the passage of the seasons. Beneath the ice walls and snow turrets of her father's castle were celebrations that Sol-stice imagined would continue forever. In an immense cavern with frost-covered walls and a ceiling that re-flected the firelight, faces glowed, arms were linked, legs spun through the steps of the ceremonial dance. Music was played far into the night. Her mother with her head thrown back, her father leaning over his wife, kissing her mouth: Solstice would always remember those things.

Each spring the Progress traveled from Winter's cas-tle to Summer's palace. They sailed on galleys with iron prows that broke the ice flows, and people on the shore held up the first green shoots.

One day when the King of Winter departed to go on a hunt, his daughter was just enough of a child to ask him if she could come too. He smiled and said no but maybe some other year. Her mother looked away and said noth-ing. She and Solstice made the next part of their journey above the land on woven gondolas born aloft by enor-mous flights of birds. They passed over a port city with walls and a citadel. Solstice remembered that it had been a seaside town with its docks all golden with harvested grain when they traveled north that autumn.

Her father never rejoined them at Summer's Palace, and her mother was sad and angry. Solstice wondered long and hard about what she had done to make all this happen. Late in that season word came to the Palace that Cronus was dying.

Solstice and her mother set out first on chariots pulled by black leopards and then on barges drawn by dolphins and whales. The sky grew dark, the earth trembled. Shepherds on hillsides, women drying wash on beaches, fishermen in their tiny boats were frightened and looked to their gods. But only Solstice glanced back.

The King of Winter was standing on the stairs of the Palace of Time when they arrived. Solstice ran to him. His wife did not. Solstice saw the coldness in their eyes. Chance saw all that happen and thought Solstice was beautiful. She was with her father Lord Folly. And because she knew that he'd always tell the truth if you took him by surprise, she asked what had happened to Winter and Summer.

"The Lord of Life persuaded Cronus who was old and unobservant to make Summer and Winter wed. For a time that seemed to keep his wife and King Winter apart. Now obviously it does not." Folly shook his head, amazed as he always was when this happened, and told her, "You must tell no one what I said."

In death Cronus was as big compared to the other Gods as they could be to mortals. His body filled the Hall of Kings. A battle shield covered each eye. Dozens of his descendants carried him from the Palace down to the sea and placed him on a golden barge. The earth shivered beneath them, waves smashed against the shore, and the marble stairs of the Palace of Time cracked in a hundred places.

The King of Oceans and the Queen of Tides pulled the barge out on the water. The clouds parted and noon sunlight streamed down. The barge erupted in flame, and a large white spark flew towards the sun.

Then the Gods and Powers slowly turned back to the Palace for a long and contentious Council meeting. The cousins, from small to almost grown, watched from the Balcony of Fair Regard. Once both her parents would immediately have looked for Solstice. Now she saw her father exchange a glance with Lady Death, saw her mother walk arm and arm with Fate and Folly while watching her husband.

Chance smiled at Solstice as all the cousins went to the Corridor of Laughter and Tears. There they opened the tabernacle containing the four elements, formed a circle, and played a game of fast toss with Earth, Air, Fire, and Water. It started slowly as a game even the smallest children could play. A gust of air was batted from hand to hand while a spinning globe went around the circle in the other direction. Then a spark and a fistful of brine appeared.

As the tossing grew faster Solstice cupped her hand to catch the water as she had once before. But this time it was icy cold. She shivered as she tossed it. "Nasty as Winter," said an older cousin, and the others laughed.

"Cold as Death," said another. Someone snickered, and Solstice saw eyes turn her way.

The game sped up. The flame was hot and had to be tossed as it was grabbed. The globe grew larger and spun so fast it was hard to control. The gust was now a stiff breeze that bit and blew into players' eyes. The tosses no longer went around the circle. Older participants threw across the space to ones younger and less prepared.

Solstice moved quickly, batted ice across the circle as fast as it came to her and slapped the invisible blast of air as hard as she could right back at the cousin who had thrown it at her. But as she did, someone sent a torch, which turned over and over as it headed her way. Solstice knocked the fire away with her hand, but instead of heading back to the other players it spun into the air. Gold filigree covered the walls and ceiling in delicate arabesques. The flame hit the wall and spurted toward the ceiling.

In amusement or horror, everyone watched. But Chance smashed the icy water against the flames, and Fire disappeared from the game. She winked at Solstice who fell in love for the first time. Then everyone heard the shouts and slamming of doors as the Council broke up and the game was forgotten.

❦

Solstice traveled back into Summer with her mother. Chance and her parents accompanied them. Mountains that Solstice had passed on the way to the funeral had been reduced to piles of rocks. Islands full of mortals had disappeared beneath the sea.

"They had a shrine to my mother in a town right here," said Solstice.

Chance said, "We felt tremors at old Cronus's death; here the earth opened up. Our misfortunes are their catastrophes."

Solstice told her friend, "Once when I was very small they put on a pageant. People dressed as Winter and Summer, as old Cronus, as me, and acted out our lives as they imagined them. I tried to make my parents stop and watch. They paused but just for a moment."

On their journey home they detoured so that the Queen of Summer could gaze upon the Gates of Death. These were bronze doors set into the mouth of a cave. Solstice watched her mother gesture in a pattern that she would never forget. Vegetation suddenly grew; vines tangled themselves all over the doors.

Fate said, "She will have to fight her way in and out of her own palace, and she will always think of you."

Folly said, "And each time she'll think less of Winter." Fate nodded but Folly remembered that Solstice was present and grimaced at his own remark.

That year's Progress from summer to winter was the first Solstice made without her parents. She and her entourage floated over mountains in hot air balloons and went down smooth roads in fast carriages. Solstice was lonely without Chance. She had become a young lady. The dwarfs and monkeys now seemed like toys to be set aside.

On the shore of an inland sea her mother's servants turned her over to her father's people. Solstice embarked on a thin new ship with huge sails that flew along the coast. As the mortal world raced past, she caught sight of a long row of scaffolds, each with a hanged man, and saw the walled city she always noticed now burned and deserted. The ship set out over open water, and when they reached the other shore, the boat dropped anchor. People saw her, and while some fell onto their knees, many stared in what might have been fear or anger.

Solstice noticed that she had to travel further than she ever had to reach her father's kingdom. When she arrived, the King of Winter was glad to see her. But Lady Death was also there, and while Death always keeps the one great secret she knows about each of us, she was not pleased to have Summer's child around her.

Toward the end of the following summer Solstice and her mother paid a visit to the Palace of Time. The Lord of Life had taken Old Cronus' place, and many were not happy with this. Solstice noticed that the fire damage to the gold filigree in The Corridor of Laughter and Tears had never been repaired.

Winter was present. He and Summer encountered each other only at Council meetings. Solstice overheard older cousins describe her mother's contempt and her father's indifference. Chance told her they were talking about things they hadn't seen.

In the Rotunda of the Great Family beneath the bas reliefs, the murals, the oil paintings of Cronus, his siblings and their descendants, the cousins played the Game of Couples. The Sybil was brought in and placed on a marble table. Bets were laid. Then the Sybil, in silk robes and turban, all jeweled moving parts and with a painted face bright as ceramic, tossed a handful of small bones in the air. The bones came down pointing like a skeleton's finger at one portrait on the walls. The Sybil picked them up and tossed them again, and the bones pointed at another portrait. These two were a couple.

Hoots and laughter rang as Lord Folly was matched with the West Wind. No one believed that. Everyone yawned when the finger pointed first at the Sun and

57

then at the Moon, that boring old couple. Amid snickers Winter and Death came up as a combination again and again. But shocked silence followed when the bones pointed first to Solstice and then to Chance. Cousins murmured when the next time the bones pointed it was first to Chance and then to Solstice.

A great sun-yellow and tropic-green glider floated on the water at the foot of the cracked marble stairs of the Palace of Time. Sea planes circled above waiting to pull the glider into the air.

"I never want to come here again," Solstice said.

"We never will," said Chance with the voice of her mother, Fate. And as she said this Solstice knew that would be so.

In something not unlike a God's year and a day later Solstice and Chance traveled toward Winter in a motorcade. They held hands. The night was clear and the moon was full. It would have been harvest time, but no crops grew in the land of roads and parking lots through which they passed.

Solstice said to her friend, "I wish mortals still came out to see us. I miss them."

At that moment Chance caught a flicker in the corner of her eye. Turning, she saw large figures—God-size and somehow familiar—moving against the sky. She immediately ordered the driver to halt.

Hundreds of cars sat in the huge drive-in, hot rods stuffed with teens, sedans with young lovers hardly looking at the screen, station wagons with parents in the front seat and the back full of pillows and blankets and kids in pajamas with feet and drop seats.

Above them, in dazzling color, the young prince with his snow white hair and ice blue eyes, the princess with her dark skin and eyes of amber bowed before a majestic greybeard while four roly-poly animated characters with their cheeks puffed out flew around them in comic elation.

Chance stood holding her hand as Solstice witnessed the flurry of images that was the animated version of her parents' marriage. She watched her own birth and presentation to the world and saw the evil queen try to destroy the marriage of Winter and Summer by kidnapping their child.

That last part made Solstice shake her head as did the ending, where everything turned out happily. While watching, she and Chance had assumed the Godlike stature of the characters on screen.

A few people—the bored parent tired of the dumb old legends, the lover waiting for her boyfriend to come back from the refreshment stand—turned around and caught a glimpse of two gigantic figures staring down. Several reported it to the theater management. Someone called the local paper.

Each time Solstice visited the land of ice and snow it was smaller and the trip was longer. When she and Chance reached The King of Winter in his castle, he himself seemed shrunken and diminished. Death was not there, though he kept saying he expected her at any moment.

Solstice thought of her mother who burned with life and anger and of how summer was slowly engulfing the world. But most of all she thought of the images she'd seen in the night and of the people who had watched them so intently.

She and Chance slept together openly for the first time. Solstice was just young enough and with just enough respect for her parents to hesitate in her father's house.

Chance smiled and said, "To those at the Palace of Time we are already a couple. But they don't know that we will be the greatest couple of all!" Chance spoke truth just like her father. But her smile was in no way rueful, and they fell onto the bed laughing.

Much later, on their Progress back to Summer it was Chance who knew the spot where they had stopped on the way to Winter's Palace. Again they arrived at night but the cars, the screen with its moving figures were gone. Nothing remained but the fragments of a paved field lost amid weeds and a few rusted metal poles that had once held speakers for each car.

The overpass behind the theater was empty of traffic. The stores on the neighboring highway stood dark in the middle of abandoned parking lots. But a cluster of lights in the distance indicated that mortals were present.

Chance found that neither Fate nor Folly had given her any wisdom that dealt with this.

Solstice stood taking in all she saw. Then with complete self-assurance she made the gesture she had seen her mother make. Trees sprouted, the land became a meadow again. She said nothing but began to walk toward the lights and the mortals who fascinated her so. Vegetation sprang up around her. Chance paused for a moment and with no certainty, for once, of what would happen, she hurried to catch up.

Illustration by Arthur Rackham for *The Rhinegold* (*The Ring of the Niblung*) by Richard Wagner, 1910

# The Lady of Wands

## 1.

October morning light it seems to me is as sweet in the Maxee neighborhood as anywhere on Heaven, Earth, or the Fairy Kingdoms. The windows in my Aerie atop the Court of Wands overlook this mongrel demi-monde in all four directions.

Sitting with my feet up on the desk on such a day, I sip a mug of Charile, the enchanted black tea that erases bad memories and hangovers. Hortense, the housekeeper, brews a pot each morning, leaves it, and disappears until I've drunk it all.

Hangovers are pretty much behind me. But a Fey woman such as I, whose life has been underway for a few centuries, will have some bad memories if her existence has held any meaning. And the tea is part of my morning ritual.

That ritual also involves deflecting mental images and reports from the telepathic Relay. For I am Leonie, Lady of Wands, chief law officer of the Maxee by appointment of his Majesty Clathurin, King beneath the Hill.

*M'Lady, fire in the Flower District… M'Lady, Mortal reported dead on Melisandre Street…*

I block them. Any telepath trying to contact me sees a shield with a gray, twisted stick. It was the symbol of my grandmother, a Forest Witch.

All day and night, every day and night, all over the Maxee, Fey law officers, the Wands, present what they have seen and heard to the minds of their nearest comrades who pass it on, till it reaches this Court, where it gets sorted. And those that seem most important are forwarded to me.

On this lovely morning I harbor a bothersome secret. On my desk is a viaculum, a frozen memory. It's a tube, brass and engraved silver, light and small enough to fit easily in the hand. In the late War, ones like this were used for everything from Royal dispatches to love notes. Each is opened by a spell devised by its creator.

Every viaculum is a piece of magic, preserving something a Fey has sensed or thought. This one was made here in Fairy but, if my informant is correct, somehow ended up in the Mortal world. Last night I tried a lot of common spells and codes, but they didn't open it.

Tiny script on the brass says, "Created at the Camp of the Royal Magicers in The Silent Woods on the fortnight day before Samhain." Each time I read it, my heart stops. It's where and when my lover Darnel was killed.

Personal viaculums hang on my wall. I pick up a simple one of wood and copper. Darnel and I made it for each other when we were young, poured our memories, and sealed it. I enact the opening spell.

It's the two of us, and he will never age. I catch the view from the Bridge of Delight where we first met, hear the cries of the baby gargoyles at Ellingstone, feel the touch of our bodies. For a few minutes I'm in the small club in Gotham listening to the song "Where or When." We went there disguised as mortals so long ago.

I want to try a spell from my grandmother on the via-culum made on the day of Darnel's death. But I'm also aware of messages from the four corners of the Maxee. I filter them, take a taste: *M'Lady a Royal Cavalcade on the Concourse of High Regard for early this noontide… M'Lady, the name of the dead Mortal male on Melisandre Street…*

Reminded of my duty, I turn and look south beyond the low buildings, twisting streets, and traffic chaos. I have a distant view of autumn trees, of hedges sculpted like unicorns and gryphons.

This is the roof of the Palace of the King beneath the Hill. All is graceful follies and elegant guard houses. Beneath it is a place of wonders, of whispering stairs and windows looking out onto the floors of oceans, a place where shadows dance and song comes out of your throat even if you resist.

Anyone in the Palace who doesn't play a double game plays a triple one. No truth is ever told, no promise is ever fully kept, even if made by the King himself. It's a better place to remember than to experience.

The din beating on my shield is like distant hail: *"M'Lady! M'Lady?"*

*"M'Lady…"*

Then a single knock sounds on my door. It's Rasia, my adjutant. I lock the viaculum in a security drawer. "Open," I say aloud. And she does, stands tall in our brown and yellow autumn uniform and dark red cape, a symbolic white wand on her belt.

As protocol demands, she dissolves her mental shield with the red falcon, offers me access to her thoughts and dreams.

As protocol demands, I refuse. No need for telepathy. I already know the mixture of ability and ambition I'd find, plus a resolve never to be this foolish when *she* becomes Lady of Wands.

And she knows my intent to use her until she's worn and tired. For her own good, of course.

The hammering on my mental shield continues. "Tell the others I'm alive and well and will deal with them."

She nods, sends the message, and the contacts abate.

Curious as to why I got a dozen messages about a dead Mortal, I open a slit in my shield and view an image from the first Wand on the scene, a male nude in a garden. I recognize the spot: the mortal was found on the grounds of Count Orland's townhouse. The face also is familiar. I was shown it last night by the informant who gave me the viaculum.

*Melisandre Street* is my order. On official duty, I travel by ground car with sirens and flashing lights. It's in imitation of a wonderment I saw in Gotham a century ago.

## 2.

The Maxee grows each year, but it's close packed. Because I can, I reach out for the constant wash of minds in this demi-monde I love.

I catch a wisp of anguish from a lovelorn Troll and a flash of anger from the Nixie she adores. I hear a snatch of the melody a young Mortal can't get out of his head and escape before it has me too. I taste spicy tomato bisque on the palate of a chef from the Faraway Hills, hear the chirping of baby finches as they sound to a Fey child too young to block my mind. A Mermaid courtesan relaxes in the bath because her lord had just departed. A Trickster boy dreams of Malfoix the actress.

Only mature Fey possess the Gift and can block me. When I touch those minds, I see the images on their mental shields: open hands signaling "stop," blank walls, closed eyes, just as they would see my silver stick. Even if I could penetrate those shields, it would be unmannerly and possibly unwise.

On my circuit I touch several Wands doing street patrol. They automatically offer entry into their minds, which I decline.

Shortly I'm on Melisandre, nicknamed, "The Gentry's Playground," looking down at the body. It lies sprawled naked on the grass under a silver linden tree trimmed in the shape of a winged lion.

Few mysteries surround mortals in a society run by telepaths. This is a fine specimen, perhaps forty, with just a few lines on his face and a touch of gray in the hair. Current fashion among the Fey finds the impending decay of Mortal beauty to be piquant.

Rasia gazes as one does at a dead pet. She'll lose this sentimentality. Wands surround the property; block any mental or physical intrusions.

The young Wand who was first on the scene shows me a faun in work clothes. *The gardener who found him. Cause of death: breath was stopped. From the looks of the ground he didn't die here; was brought and laid out.*

*Any memories left?*

This Wand is good at his work. I feel the brief moment of suffocation and the death throes caught in the victim's disappearing memory.

*Last sights, last thoughts?* I ask. In the moments after death the brain is still full of images and memories. Sometimes Mortals are killed because they saw something they shouldn't have.

*Orland's house servants summoned us when they discovered the body. But he'd been dead for an hour or more.*

I'm shown a moment of utter darkness. His last thought was: *It's not the time…,* which is common.

*His name was Tangent Phillips*, the Wand tells me and pauses to look at something to my left.

I've already felt the presence. I turn and see the elongated, slender figure, the flickering of the Glamour, the thin mustache and chin beard in the current mode. A small entourage stands a few yards behind him.

*Count Orland.* I bow from the neck.

*M'lady.* He does the same. His expression is one of sincere regret. "I've never seen him before. It's a pity."

I smile to indicate that goes without saying. Unspoken is that it would make no sense for him to do this. Count Orland is on the rise, a rival to Lord Nightwood, the Chancellor.

For a Fey grandee to slay a mortal isn't a crime of great consequence. But it would reflect badly on his name—as if he'd cut the wings off a flying horse, or killed a unicorn for its horn. In any case, unless it's for treason, a Fey grandee's mind cannot be investigated.

Like any good cop, I have my street contacts. One called Minimum, who gave me the viaculum last night, got it from a Mortal who'd just smuggled it into Fairy.

Minimum thought it had something to do with the rivalry of young Orland and Nightwood.

The Count bows again and retires to his townhouse. The question is who gains by this and how. I check the Relay; images of Phillips dead in the Garden have been seen by Fey at several government agencies. The Palace itself has looked. I check more closely. A low-level equerry has seen them several times.

Melisandre Street is on a hill. The dead Mortal being rolled into a shroud makes me look north beyond the buildings of the Maxee to the ancient forest we call The Veil. Above The Veil I make out the broken towers of Gotham, wavering in sunlight like the mirage they are. Tangent Phillips crossed into the Maxee from that direction.

## 3.

At the border mortals seeking entry are examined. It's where I go to find out how he did it.

Standing at the end of the Fairy Road, I gaze at the gigantic Gryphon and Dragon that flank it on either side. These are the first things mortals see when they find their way here. The Road was the path down which the Fey first traveled when we deserted our Mortal cousins eons ago. The statues were here even then. The route between Earth and Fairy is hard for Mortals to find. It passes through The Veil, the Old Forest. And woe betides any who try to leave this path. Even in daylight, spirits walk howling out of the shadows, and birds long dead fly at a Mortal's eyes.

Only the stout of heart, the fugitives, thrill seekers, and lunatics continue on. What they find, past the statues, are an antique custom house filled with bureaucrats ranging from Tree Druids to Sprites, a small Wand station, and what looks like a temple.

This last is the Chamberlains' court, where Fey plumb the travelers' minds and pass judgment on who gets to enter and who gets to leave.

The thoughts and memories of the one who judged each refugee are recorded and preserved. I sit in Chamberlain Semeresia's office. She fought in the Battle of the Giants' Fall nine centuries ago. She's in judicial black, tall with skin as white as her hair. Semeresia handled Tangent Phillips and gave him a visa.

*I remember the case*, she tells me. *It was only yesterday afternoon.* My guess is her memory has been questioned lately. But the face she recollects and shows me is that of the man whose corpse I saw.

Her clerk, a middle aged Sylph, appears holding a small office viaculum with Phillips records. Looking into it I see him turn 360 degrees, first clothed then not.

Semeresia had extracted a life history from his mind. Raised in Gotham, thirty-nine years old, lived by his wits, a bit of a scoundrel, dealt in rare objects.

*Or what they consider rare objects*, she tells me. *He carried a sack of them.* They were emptied onto a table for her inspection: Jewelry, a crucifix, small artworks. One image catches my attention: the viaculum now locked in my desk.

*I didn't especially notice it among the Mortal clutter*, Semeresia answers when I point it out. *I heard what happened to him*, she adds, *mischief among the Gentry. That's what brings you down here. No wars to keep them busy like we had, hey M'Lady?* She asks with a rusty chuckle.

*Absolutely, your honor*, I reply.

In the car, Rasia shows me the Sylph clerk telling her, *Chamberlain Semeresia only hears cases when other Chamberlains are sick or it's very busy. Count Orland was gracious enough to use his influence to keep her at her post.*

Then I see and hear the clerk say, *Yesterday afternoon we got the order to prepare a case at the last minute.*

*By whose order?* Rasia asks, and the clerk says, *From the Palace is all I know.*

Rasia says aloud. "She wonders how much longer Chamberlain Semeresia will be on duty here. Wonders about a job at the Court of Wands."

"She's not very discreet," I remark, and we're both amused. My private question is who gained by having this unobservant judge.


4.


When we reach twisting, traffic-choked Bonne Fee Street I get out of the cruiser, send Rasia back to handle routine matters. She takes off with sirens blaring as I start to walk.

Secrets are rare things in a world full of mind readers. Only the powerful or the isolated have them. Casting about I feel Imps with brains like rat nests slide past me bound on dirty errands. Pixies sell contraband. Produce vans made of parts of old Mortal vehicles jostle jitneys painted in bright greens and reds on the narrow street lined with odd old buildings. Mortals hang out on the corners waiting to catch a Fey's glance. Some look my way. They come to the Maxee on the run from a world falling apart and discover that however tough or smart, whatever their accomplishments on Mortal Earth, only their amusing, vulnerable bodies are of interest to their new overlords. Tangent Phillips had a bit more.

I cast my mind wide. I'm sure it's already known that M'Lady is walking. I do it often enough that informants expect it.

Several who approach me I bat away. Then in front of me is the figure I most want to see. Huffing along Sweet Music Street where it crosses Bon Fee, studiously not looking in my direction, is Minimum. He's tall for a Gnome but short and stocky by any other standard. His mouth is working, and I imagine the wheezing breaths, the mumbled string of complaints, and the prayers to the guiding spirits of his people. I turn onto Sweet Music in the same direction as his, walking half a block behind him.

*We meet again*, I tell him. He's used to my entering the surface of his mind. I don't go further.

"Greetings M'Lady. I trust the day finds you well." Oddly, Minimum is always formal.

Among veterans of The War of the Elf King's Daughter, there's camaraderie. Botched marriage negotiations led to a conflict between Elf and Fey as nasty, for all the Glamour on display and all the odes written by bards who managed to miss the action, as any fought anywhere.

*How goes it?* I scan around us to see if anyone listens. No one does.

He lets me see what's on his mind. "Nightwood's minions treat us like scum. They lost my disability plea. All I want is what was promised when they conscripted me. If only his Majesty knew."

I've heard all this before. Like many in the Maxee, he believes in the King, hates Nightwood, and has hopes for Orland. Minimum has ties to underground groups, which makes him useful to me.

The mind of a Gnome is a gnarled and difficult place. I could enter it forcibly, but doing so would end any friendship and respect between two beings. I show him Tangent Phillips and the viaculum. *Only in the Maxee a few hours when he gave you this. How did he know you?*

Minimum squirms like he wants to drill a hole in the pavement with the base of his spine and tries to quicken his walk. But I stop his legs from moving.

*Whoever sent him to you knew you'd give this to me. Once he did he was killed. Was it Orland's people? Nightwood's? Someone else?*

Minimum shakes his head. He's made a point of not knowing and fears for his life if he tries to find out. I give him the money I have with me and tell him to hide until I send word not to.

Then I continue my walk. As it turns out, the next one to get in touch with me is another old war comrade.

Ancient, narrow Bon Fee Street eventually empties into The Concourse of High Regard, which cuts through the Maxee from north to south. Today, a Royal Cavalcade to welcome the Queen of the Fortunate Isles is scheduled, and a traffic jam is underway. Skimming minds, I pick up drivers' thoughts: "Cursed by the gods to travel among creatures of myth and madness!" and "What'll go first, my brakes or my brains?" Young Wands lay their minds on Mortal truckers and Goblin cycle messengers, get tourist jitneys full of visiting Nymphs and Satyrs from the Faraway to unload their passengers, make vehicles blocks away turn onto side streets. They are aware of my presence and work hard. This part of the job bores me. But in the distance, I hear trumpets, drums, and beating wings. I pause: from childhood on I've loved a parade.

Down the avenue I see sleek green and silver cars floating toward me on clouds of Glamour. Royal Guards in blue and silver ride escort above them on winged horses. Cheers echo against the buildings.

The Queen of the Fortunate Isles is a small, plump, not terribly fortunate looking lady. But Clathurin, King beneath the Hill, makes up for that. Big, smiling at the crowd, he has the gift of letting each one think he notices and cares for them. Mortals and the other lesser residents of the Maxee live here at his whim.

Lord Nightwood, the Chancellor, rides with the Fortunate Isles Foreign Secretary. His narrow face sags, and he looks as if he's suffered a bad loss. The love given to the king is balanced by hatred for his advisor. Some even dare to boo him.

A beating of wings makes me look up as a figure in a Marshall's uniform descends. Nadelier was a captain to my lieutenant in his Majesty's Relayers. Now she commands the Royal Guards and wears enough medals that I'm surprised her horse can get off the ground, even with magic.

Hooves clatter on the pavement. Humans, sprites, a Dryad, turn from the Cavalcade to see. Nadelier smiles. *His majesty is gratified that you're out walking a beat, keeping us safe, M'Lady.*

I too smile and ask, *Is that the whole message Commandant?*

Nadelier nods and looks serious. Her real message is that his Majesty thought of me just now.

The Chancellor looks like he's suffered a loss. The King is curious and perhaps more. I wonder what each knows about Phillips and the viaculum.

I thank Nadelier and stand back as the huge wings beat and the horse rises in the air. Once she and I were as close and frank as combat makes two beings. Life at the Palace has turned her into an enigmatic creature.

## 5.

Back in my Aerie, I go immediately to the desk and put the viaculum in an inside pocket. From another drawer I take a wand once owned by my grandmother, the Witch. These days Fey Wands are decorative. The magic is mostly mental. For a Witch they're where the magic lies.

For the rest of the afternoon, I pick at a lunch Hortense prepared and wrap myself in routine. I block all other matters as I monitor the Relay. I see blackened binbery trees from a fire set in Bane Woods Park; witness crane trucks with golem crews hauling away a demolished van and a slightly damaged bus on Morgana Way. I watch Wands subdue a rural Fey squire who ran amok at the Tintigal Tavern. None of this need concern me, but I take my time with each.

A report to which I return shows a mortal woman who told a Wand she saw Tangent Phillips in the company of Count Orland yesterday evening. But while she certainly saw Orland, the mortal wasn't Phillips. My interest is in who else has looked. The Palace has seen it several times: the equerry again, a military adjutant twice. Covering for superiors, perhaps.

A polite relay from His Majesty's secretary says, "I have been told to inquire after a certain investigation."

I ignore it and scan a series of Wands' faces. I'm told who they are and why they're on the promotion list. I consider each one, question a couple, and approve the rest.

Once or twice I turn the viaculum in my hand. Try to work out by what twists of conspiracy it came to me and why. I believe Orland had Phillips killed and left in his own garden. If I'm correct, it was a message to Nightwood that he had intercepted Tangent Phillips and this viaculum.

At dusk a Relay comes from the Palace with the Royal Seal and a direct request for a report on the incident at Orland's townhouse. His Majesty must know about the viaculum and where it went.

## 6.

Moving quickly, I exit the Court of Wands, hail a cab, and am driven to the mouth of an old alley within a block of The Veil. It's dark as I glide over cobblestones and make a right at a windowless warehouse. I always go to the Oldest Forest for privacy. Proper Fey, however they deny it, are wary of this place. But not witches.

Beyond are shadows and trees under a full moon. My wand's a beautiful thing, dark wood that catches moonlight. I hold my left palm open, keep the wand in my right, and recite aloud the simple chant that any witch child learns.

"One oh one, the goddess walking,"

And The Veil parts.

"Two oh two, I show my hand,"

Which I do in the proper way.

"Three oh three, with no stopping,"

A rough path appears before me.

"Four oh four, I find this land."

The next verses are not to be shared. Holding my wand, I bow before the ghost trees, and the gloom of The Veil lightens somewhat.

Ghosts of The Veil, Fey, Human, Other, give me wide birth. My wand guides me through the maze. I turn west and avoid the mumbling bog; take a sharp north away from the grove of green light. I head to a place I know, a glade with a great gray tree at the center. I sit under it in autumn moonlight.

Spells had been cast over the years to open this viaculum. I sense them. They failed. No one has gazed into this since it was created. Under the moon, I work every piece of unbinding magic I know. Move my hands, do the ritual poses, chant, "Light in the dark, shade in the noontide, salt in the honey, sweetness in the sea…" and all the rest.

None of it unseals the viaculum.

I turn it over in my mind. The viaculum is valuable enough for individuals to suborn Chamberlains' Court and flaunt a murdered Mortal. No Magicers survived that day. But at least one Fey believes he knows the contents: The Chancellor? The Count? The King?

I close my eyes and think of Darnel. It would be heartbreaking, but I hope to get one last sight of him.

It's unlikely he created this piece and meant it for me. But we shared a code. That view from the bridge, the baby gargoyles, the touch of our bodies, the song "Where or When": I put those memories in proper order, keep my dreams and fears in check, raise the viaculum to my eyes, hardly dare to open them.

My heart jumps. I'm in the viaculum, floating like a breeze. Figures stand on the edge of a forest in the black and gold uniform of the Magicers. One of them is Darnel, young, alive, and part of the regimental Relay.

More and more figures come into view. Darnel stands on the edge of the Silent Woods. His smile is wonderful. In one hand he holds this viaculum. Under his other arm is his hawk, Tamil. His message is to me. *Dearest Leonie! We hope each day will be the one that ends this horror.*

In fact, this day would be the end of them. Surprise? Betrayal? No one knows how they all died. I want to touch them, to warn them. I want to scream aloud.

*We are honored! His Majesty himself has paid an unannounced visit!* Skipping from one mind to another, Darnel shows me Clathurin, young and smiling. No account ever mentioned his presence. All, in fact, describe him at the Gates of Thunder fifty miles away, learning of the annihilation of his favorite regiment.

Knowing the outcome makes this hard, but I have to watch. The sudden death of pickets goes through the Relay like a shock. The Elvin attack is immediate: thousands of minds smothering the Magicers. Through Darnel I see Clathurin, eyes wide with fear, jump on his winged horse. Nightwood looking terrified, and a few retainers are with him. They're in the air and flying away before anyone else can react.

The Magicers cover his retreat. As he shows me this, minds batter Darnel's shield, break it, choke him, and twist his ganglia, his limbic system. I feel Darnel snap the viaculum onto Tamil's leg and toss the hawk into the air. It never reached me. Everything goes black, and I catch his last thought, *It's not the time…*

## 7.

In the first light I exit The Veil. Part of the night was spent watching Darnel, seeing him young and hopeful again and again. The rest was spent destroying his viaculum.

The Wand Relay finds me almost immediately. I'm proud of them. Before I've gotten two blocks, Rasia is there with the cruiser and the siren. She's clearly been up all night. Her concern touches me, though part of it is worry about her own career.

*M'Lady. A Royal Summons!*

*As expected*, I assure her. Rasia wants to take me to the Palace immediately. I refuse and return us to The Court of Wands. On the way I contact Hortense who is, of course, awake and ask her to prepare. I also connect with Eliad at the Restoration Day and Night Glamour Parlor. The sprite, his tiny wings aquiver, waits for us on the sidewalk in front of the Court.

A hundred minds want contact with me. I bat them away. Upstairs Hortense has my full dress uniform with cape and the boots with diamond spurs laid out. With her help and a generous dousing of glamour and costume suggestions from Eliad I appear fit for the presence of a King. Where I'm headed, appearance is everything.

We drive to the outer guard posts and are waved through. At the foot of the Hill Nadelier waits in full uniform to accompany me. Old war camaraderie enters into it, I know, but also the fact she is one of the few of high enough rank to take me into custody if that proves necessary. *I assured His Majesty he could rely on you*, she tells me, which means my loyalty was questioned.

We don't come to the Royal Presence via the Stairs of High Regard amidst trumpets and triumphant murals. But neither am I taken down the Corridor of Sighs, where one hears the Sad Pavane and is flanked by casements overlooking the garden of sobbing trees.

Instead my path is via the plain, neutral Gallery of Light. His Majesty meets me in what looks like the library of a country house complete with flames dancing in the fireplace. Nadelier stops and closes the doors behind me. No sound, no telepathy enters here.

Clathurin smiles as I curtsy, says, "Dear Leonie," and waves me to a seat. Then: *We are old friends.*

I know a king has no friends, but I bow my head at the honor. He motions me to keep my seat and stands up, tall and majestic. Everything about him seems false to me now.

"All his subjects' lives are a King's responsibility. The lives lost that day are most directly so since it was me the enemy was after." I wonder about the elaborate alibi he and Nightwood constructed and what happened to the attendants who accompanied them.

"The King's safety is the duty of his subjects," I find myself telling him.

He shows me his memory of Darnel creating the viaculum. My heart turns over at the sight. He speaks quietly.

"I regret my panic, the lies I told. I've wondered ever since whether this survived. Then early today I learned that a viaculum with that date had been brought into the city.

"When I found it had been given to you. I was glad it would be opened by someone I could trust."

I show him how I destroyed it. He looks me in the eye. I see images of the Royal Family. *Better the known evil is what you decided. My Queen is dead, my brother is an idiot, and my son will be a silly boy, however long he lives.*

Those had been my thoughts.

*Only you and I know,* the King tells me. I think of Nightwood, and Clathurin shakes his head. *The Chancellor left his life last evening by his own decision.*

King and Chancellor had been welded together for decades. Nightwood must have known the King was about to eliminate him. Desperate, he smuggled the viaculum from the Mortal World to the Kingdom, saw it through Semeresia's court, only to lose it in the back streets of the Maxee.

His suicide perhaps came when he realized it was in my hands. That was Orland's doing. Not sure what the viaculum contained but hoping it discredited Nightwood, he allowed Phillips to pass it to me via the dissidents before having him killed.

The King is silent for a long moment, stares out at the autumn garden. Now only he and I know the secret. I have faced death before.

"You will succeed Nightwood," he says aloud. "This will be wildly popular."

My loyalty is proven. My life is spared. But she who serves the king shares the lies of the king, and he won't let me far out of his sight.

I feel dread as I rise and bend a knee. *As your majesty wishes.*

Word travels fast in a court of telepaths. Nadelier greets me when I step back into the Gallery of Light. Courtiers, beautifully dressed, wait in my path and smile discreetly.

I think about the lost comfort of my mornings in the Aerie and of all that must be done. Before that, though, I will create a secret viaculum and hide it as only I know how to do. It will show the events of the last two days, beginning with October light and ending right here.

Illustration by Arthur Rackham for *The Valkyrie (The Ring of the Niblung)* by Richard Wagner, 1910

Illustration by Arthur Rackham for
*Cinderella* by C. S. Evans, 1919

# The Bear Dresser's Secret

Early one morning Sigistrix the Bear Dresser left the Duchess and her castle. He gave no warning before he slammed the golden tricorn hat, the sign of a Grand Master of the Animal Dressers Guild, onto his head and picked up his suitcase.

He gave no reason, though as he walked through the gates he did remark to Grismerelda, the Duchess's young maid, "A Bear Dresser answers to no one." She watched the many snowy egret feathers on the Grand Master's hat flutter in the breeze as he disappeared into the dawn.

The Duchess was having her hair done when they told her. "Faster, faster, silly girl," she said. "Today is a disaster and I must look my very best." Every morning Grismerelda spent hours getting her dressed and ready.

"It's just like a Bear Dresser to leave like this. Dear Grandfather Fernando the Mad would have known how to handle him." She enjoyed reminiscing about her distinguished ancestors. Who among us doesn't?

She summoned her chamberlain, her guard captain, and her jester. "You see what must be done," she told them. "The bears have no one to dress them, and the Great Fair is one month from today."

"Yes, your grace," said the chamberlain.

"He never looked trustworthy to me," said the guard captain.

"Take my life, please," said the jester.

"We have entered our bears in the animal costume competition from time out of mind," said the Duchess. "And with a few highly regrettable exceptions, such as occurred last year, we have always won first prize. And we will continue to do so.

"Sigistrix always dressed bears for me. His father dressed them for my father. His grandfather dressed them for mine, except for those times he escaped and had to be brought back in a cage. These things were much more easily handled in the old days before they had laws.

"I expect results from you three by his evening, or I will be most ANNOYED. And you all know what that means."

Indeed they did. The three were deathly silent for a moment. Then the chamberlain cried, "Gentlemen, to the bear's house."

Meanwhile the bears themselves, large and small, brown, black, and white, were at home dressed in their natural fur.

"Good morning, bears. Always lovely to see you," said the chamberlain and kissed several paws.

"Ten-hut!" said the captain.

"A funny thing happened on the way to my beheading," said the jester.

But, though they worked hard all day and ruined several satin cummerbunds, a dozen pairs of silver slippers and a tailored tweed skirt, the bears were not dressed at nightfall.

"This will NEVER do," the Duchess said. "My god-mother, The Countess Freluchia, would have had you all beaten soundly and hung up by your thumbs!"

For weeks the three men tried to dress the bears. Every morning after breakfast it would start. They begged them to put on elbow length gloves; they tried to wrestle them into velvet knee britches and satin far-thingales and did high-step cakewalks to show them how fine it was to wear dancing shoes. Each evening the bears still were not dressed. Everyone was very unhappy.

One day the Duchess decided to dress the bears her-self. "I, her grace the Duchess, command that you all become dressed," she said.

But nothing happened.

"I shall close my eyes, and when I open them you will all be dressed."

When she did, nothing happened.

"I shall give each of you a jar of honey."

Nothing happened (though the bears liked honey very much).

"Uncle Rodney of the Bloody Hand had an instinct for dealing with stubborn animals. He once had a pig put in the stocks for failing to bow to him."

The bears wandered away.

"Just like bears! Come Grismerelda, I must go and dress for lunch." And she stomped back to the castle.

That evening while getting the Duchess dressed for bed, Grismerelda asked a question that had bothered her.

"Your grace, how did Sigistrix dress the bears?"

"It was an old animal dresser secret, handed down in his family. Mind the comb, silly girl. It's pulling my hair. You're fortunate I don't mind that as much as my dear mama did."

Grismerelda hardly dared to ask the next question. "Your grace, might I try to dress the bears?"

"Silly girl, you have no experience dressing the bears. You have only dressed me."

But next evening, when the bears still were not dressed, the Duchess remembered her maid. "Young Grismerelda wants to dress the bears. Let her try."

So the next morning, after dressing the Duchess, the maid set out to dress the bears. It was long and tiring work since bears are very hard to dress—shoes, for instance, even open-toed sandals—are extremely difficult because of the claws. And about silk stockings and bow ties it is best not even to speak.

By the end of the day she had managed to wrestle the smallest and most cooperative bear into a sundress.

"That," said the Duchess "Is not good enough. I will give you one more chance. And if you fail, I shall be forced to do to you the very thing second cousin Honoria did to the footman who dropped the butter dish."

Next day was the same. Although the bears were fond enough of Grismerelda who had sometimes brought them honey, they remained impossible to dress. She knew the Duchess would be displeased, and her mother had told her the terrible tale of Tom the footman and the troublesome butter dish and how he had walked strangely forever after the thing that was done to him.

She took out a handkerchief and wiped away a tear.

Every bear picked up a handkerchief too.

Grismerelda stopped crying. She even started to smile. "Oh bears," she said. "Thank you very much." And she reached down and picked up a hat.

By dinnertime, every bear, from the oldest in a battered French yachting cap, to the youngest in a broken propeller beanie, was wearing a hat.

"Not enough, silly girl. Who ever heard of prizes for just wearing hats?" asked the Duchess. "The judges last year called the bears' hats, 'Lacking in presence.' Still, I suppose it is something."

"Your grace," said Grismerelda, "I will have the bears dressed and ready for the fair. But I can do no other work. No one can bother me. No one can watch me. If you agree to that, the bears will be dressed. I promise."

"One does not make 'deals' with me. Why I remember the presumptuous tailor who dared to offer me a dress so fine only one of my rank could see it. I could, of course, see it and was appalled at the shoddiness of the material. His thumbs still hang over the fireplace in the autumn parlor." She paused then said, "Very well." Only the next day did she wonder who would dress *her*.

Next day bright and early Grismerelda went to the bears' house. She waited until she had their attention, and then she picked up a shoe and put it on.

It took a while, but by that evening, all the bears were wearing shoes.

Meanwhile the Duchess was dressing herself. Often she was surprised by the results. Her hair was a wild tangle. Birds thought to nest in it. In the ancestral closets, she found a turban. It had belonged to the Caliph Mustafa the Damned, a distant relative. He had lived in the castle briefly after he was exiled and before he was drawn and quartered.

She put it on her head. "Grismerelda, bring me my mirror, silly girl," she cried before remembering that Grismerelda was far too busy.

A week later her maid returned and said, "Perhaps, your grace, we would do better in the competition if the bears had better clothes."

"Wherever would we find them on such short notice, you insolent child."

Grismerelda pointed to the Duchess' closets. Later that day as they opened the tenth or eleventh trunk, the Duchess gave a little cry of recognition.

"That sea shell embroidered four piece bathing suit belonged to Nadine the Neckless, Countess of Lethe, First Lady of the Towels at the Imperial Court." The Duchess hesitated before handing it over then said, "She married my great-great-grand uncle and was an in-law, so you may take that.

"And those very long-tailed shirts belonged to my father's distant cousin Sir Douglass the Pantless—a disgraceful relic, take them.

"But you can't have that tasseled silk strangling scarf. It belonged to my dear mother," giggled the Duchess girlishly. "She used to threaten everyone with it. I will wear it in her memory, tied around my waist.

"Oh, and my dear Papa the Duke's tiny branding iron! He would heat it over a candle and sear his crest into the behinds of people who fell asleep at dinner. I'd forgotten about it!

"Those green galoshes with the frogs' heads on the toes, on the other hand, look just right for a bear. Such a large size, I can't think who they were for.

"And a box of garter belts with the ancestral crest, an amorous gargoyle, on each. There are enough for each bear to have one."

Bright and early on the morning of the fair, the bears were dressed in picture hats and silver cuirasses and silk tutus and velvet knee britches and patent leather slippers and flowing silk ties. Old father bear stuffed his feet into cowboy boots with silver spurs.

The most popular event each year was the animal costume competition. Every aristocratic house participated. That year the crowds were larger than ever, and there were many contestants.

Among them were the elephants of Countess Barzuki with a new Celtic dance routine, the swans of the Marquise de Cruel on roller skates and last year's winner, the lions of Prince Nasty wearing shoes with mirrors on them and wide brimmed picture hats lined with lighted candles.

But this year those seemed like vulgar gimmicks. Everyone agreed that the bears of the Duchess in their remarkable wardrobes were in a class by themselves.

The chief judge turned out to be Sigistrix. He smiled as he awarded first prize to the Duchess, who seemed overwhelmed.

Then, on Grismerelda's head, Sigistrix placed the copper tricorn of a master of the Animal Dressers' Guild. It bore a single egret feather, the sign of a first place finish.

From then on in the bears' house the bears dressed themselves.

And at the castle, the Duchess dressed herself.

The Duchess never learned Grismerelda's secret.

"Uncle Phineas the Unwashed did something quite horrible as a lesson to a servant who kept secrets," said the Duchess. But she was so busy trying on the many-armed hunting jacket that had once belonged to her godfather, the Elector Konrad who was nicknamed "The Octopus," that she couldn't remember what the horrible thing was.

Illustration by Arthur Rackham ("The Dragon of the Hesperides") for *Arthur Rackham's Book of Pictures*, 1913

# Sir Morgravain Speaks of Night Dragons and Other Things

There was a man I knew, a knight full worthy and brave. I forget his name, but if he's alive again somewhere in Avalon perhaps he remembers it. This knight said that we're born with a certain amount of courage and it's as well not to use it up all at once. Because I kept his piece of wisdom in mind, I still have a bit of the tiny store of courage with which I started out.

Sleep is the occupation here in Avalon. Under the spell of Queen Morgana, King Arthur and his knights slumber the years away and have rare moments of wakefulness and waiting.

I alone am mostly awake. I don't know how long I've been here. But lately, unlike the others, I sleep at what seem regular intervals, awaken in my monk-like cell, and then walk about as I'm doing now.

I tell this to you, the human faces without bodies that float before me like a vision. You resemble neither angels nor demons; you don't speak but appear to listen to what I say. Occasionally I see one or two of you following other knights in these halls. They take no note of you and know not what I'm talking about when I mention you. No one else do you follow so constantly or in such numbers as you do me. I don't know if I'm blessed or cursed.

Now coming down the corridor I see Sir Percival: the purest knight who ever lived and well aware of it.

Hello Percival, you're awake too? It's been a long time. I was talking to good old Merlin when I last woke up, and I told him I wondered how long we've all been in this endless rest. He told me he had calculated that it was getting close to two millennia.

Afraid I don't understand quite how he arrived at that, and I imagine he's asleep somewhere and can't be roused. But I find myself awake again, and I can't stop wondering if it's possible that he was right. What do you think, Percival?

Yes, I agree. The way the joints feel when you try to get out of bed makes you sure you've slept for hundreds of years. That strikes me as a better gauge than Merlin's calculations.

Can't remember my name? Well why should you have to, dear fellow? It's such a bother remembering peoples' names. Everyone should be able to remember his own name and not expect others to do it for him. I remember mine, mostly. Even at my age. As I'm sure you remembered yours even before I addressed you.

I was on my way downstairs to see if there was a cup of tea, perhaps a horn of honeyed mead to be had in the kitchens. See if anyone else is awake and wants to talk. Why don't you come along?

We'll use these stairs. I always go down this way so as to pass the royal chamber. I make it a point to peer in and view His Majesty. Each time I do I think that he almost looks like he's made of marble, a crown on his head, a scepter in one hand, and a sword in the other, a gentle rise and fall of his chest.

You know, Percival, whenever I meet someone I haven't seen in a long while as has just happened with you, I ask if they've seen His Majesty awake in this place or if they've ever spoken to anybody who has.

Myself, I've never seen him awake, nor has anyone I've talked to. You haven't either? I'm surprised. I'd have thought if it was anybody it would be one like you who saw the Grail who would have seen him.

I do remember once when we were both awake, Pellinor saying to me that he believed there are times when we are all asleep and that then the King awakens and walks among us.

Yes, I know old Pellinor thinks such a terribly mixed assortment of things! But it is possible.

Look, the doors of the Royal chamber are open, and there is his Majesty awaiting the call to arise and reclaim his crown. Notice that the bedclothes are disturbed as though he's turned in his sleep. It's said he will arise when Britain and the world are again in great danger. Perhaps he is waking up bit by bit. But I can't be sure.

No sense in lingering once you've seen King Arthur. Morgana Le Fey and her sorceress sisters do not appreciate idle curiosity or any other kind.

The stairs leading to the kitchen are right here. Be careful going down as there's no railing. We'll just pass through the Great Hall here and into the kitchens.

It's here in the Hall that I last saw the Queen. In sleep as in all things her ways are not the same as those of the rest of us. She apparently is awake a considerable amount of the time. I've seen her often when I've been up. That last time when I passed through on my way to the kitchen, just as we're doing now, there was music.

Her majesty was here and a certain knight. I think we both know which one; and it was just those two all alone. They danced a stately dance in their… what do the heathen Turks call them, pajamas? So taken with each other were they that they never noticed anyone watching.

Now I understand that the knight in question is human and that we all have failings; though I believe you rather famously do not, Percival. I understand that he is the greatest knight of us all. And Guinevere is our King's lady and deserving of our devotion for his sake. Yes I do bear those things in mind. And no I don't believe I'm mistaken. What I saw, was what I saw.

And I don't think I am spreading sordid gossip. I'm sorry, Sir Knight, that you have taken it that way. Yes, I am amazed that I'm here and in this company also. I'm surprised that I didn't awaken amidst fiery torments. Surprised that hasn't happened with many of us, in truth.

Except possibly for Galahad and the King himself, you're the one I'm least amazed to find here. And I regret that anything I said disturbed you as much as it obviously has.

And with that off goes Percival in that nightshirt with his coat of arms on front and back. It is my hope that he will remember this through any number of sleeps and that it will prey on him greatly. Since I can't think of any reason for finding myself in this exalted company, I have decided I've been put here to be myself and spread unease. Apparently honor is not completely dead inside me, though, since I have a bit of regret at offending even so sanctimonious a prig.

The truth is I saw little of the Queen back in Camelot and haven't seen her or any other woman since I've been here. No one has, I think. Morgana and the other enchantresses have reserved this place for foolish men alone.

I see a score of faces, male and female, pink English, Dark Moor, Mongol, and ones I do not know. You float about me as if listening to a minstrel in a great hall; seem to lean forward like the crowd at a jousting tournament.

I believe it interests you when I talk to others as I did just now. When I repeat another knight's words you nod, which is why I do it. You congregate when those conversations happen.

Ah, who do I see heading this way!

---

Sir Bors! Yes Percival had to hurry off as you saw. Said he needed to say his prayers. Of course I remember you dear sir and no, it's not because you're a bore. Your name stands out as do you.

My name? It blends in with all the other names at the bottom of the list. In the great days in the castle at Camelot I was down there with Sir Petipace and Sir Plenorius and the rest. It's said all are equal at a Round Table. That's a pleasant myth.

I was just about to pop into the pantry, see if there's something to soothe my nerves. It's strange to complain when we sleep away the centuries, but I couldn't stay in bed.

You also? Were you bothered by dreams about dragons? I often am. My dreams, though, are not about those fierce beasts one used to fight, which breathed fire and required a pure heart to defeat.

In the old days I used to awaken out of dreams where one of those was bearing down on me and I would suddenly realize that my heart was not pure at all.

But no, I dream of those little creatures that run around under the bed. They're the ones my nurse used to call Night Dragons when I was small. You nod, so I guess yours did the same. Remember as a boy being told they'd find you, nip your feet, and bite your toes off if you got out of bed at night?

I do recall a knight, Sir Lambegus I believe, one of the Round Table but down at my end. It seems he got up at an untimely hour, and the Night Dragons took him. Had him by the ankles and whisked him right under the bed. Witnesses heard that little chuckling sound they make. Later when they gingerly pulled up the spread there was nothing under the bed but a button or two from his clothes and one index finger.

Enough to make a man's blood run cold, I agree. Ah, here we are. Let me lead you through these kitchens with their great, cold fireplaces and rusted ox spits. Through this door is an amazing place that changes each time I visit.

Some years ago in here a chest full of ice kept food preserved. Now we have these white closets with large doors and when you open them the cold billows out like a mob of snow crones is holding convocation inside.

Ah, cocoa bubbling away on the stove! There's nothing like hot chocolate for putting you back to sleep. Care to join me? Pull up a stool.

It was in this very pantry that I saw the Lady Lynette, you know, the one who came to the court of

Camelot to beg the king to help her sister recover her realm. She was a great favorite of everyone, but she and I were quite close those many years ago.

When I saw her here she sat right where you are now in a diaphanous kind of night clothing, holding a tiny cup in her hands and singing a passing melodious roundelay to herself.

I had been looking for ale—the old kind that you chewed as you drank. There was none to be had. The ones who maintain this pantry don't go in for the old ways. But I forgot that when I saw her. It was like a thousand years or whatever it was hadn't passed, and we were back in that time when many men courted her and I was one of several who had her.

She must have felt it too. She arose as I approached. And then with few words and fewer gestures we were on the table making such a go of it. And when it was over, she arose and wrapped a silken cloak around herself and left me. And it was as if I was still asleep and in a dream. That was many sleeps and awakenings ago, and I haven't seen her since.

It was one of those old wooden tables, softened by centuries of use. These new ones are hard as marble, and I can't imagine rutting on...

Oh, I'm sorry Sir Knight. You were one of those who worshipped her in a pure manner? To you she was a fountain of innocence and hope?

Well, my compliments. You're a better knight and a better man than I or any of the others who had her. Gawain was one of those and Bedivere among many. You think I'm defiling her name? And demand satisfaction? Well you shall have it sir. Send your squire around to see mine, and it shall be arranged. Next time we're both awake.

Which I can assure him will not be soon. It hardly needs to be said that a man who stamps off without finishing hot chocolate as rich as this must be upset indeed. He will stew on this before falling back into slumber. And that is my role as I've come to understand it—to trouble the sleep of King Arthur's Knights.

At first I thought you faces were heavenly visions. Later I thought you might be from Satan. Now I'm not sure you don't follow another master entirely. The miraculous pantry is, I think, your work.

I don't know for certain that I'm not, in fact, damned and in Hell. But even if I am it is not thus far unpleasant, and I'll make the most of it as I have always tried to do with everything. Lady Lynette is an example. Our fling was long ago and far away, but lying about it just now brought it back to me in all its fine deception.

Is that you, Sir Caradoc, staring at me? My name? Well why should you have to remember other peoples' names for them I always say. It's enough that you can remember your own.

Morgravain? Yes, I believe you're right. That is my name. There's something else you're trying to remember—something about me? Well there is that poem:

I had a little nut tree
Nothing would it bear
But a silver nutmeg
And a golden pear

The King of Spain's Daughter
Came to visit me
All for the sake
Of my little nut tree

No sir, I am NOT rattling on to try and put you off your train of thought and stop you remembering something about me. The mead you've been drinking will do that well enough.

The poem is true. The tree had been in the family for generations. It was magic, though not of my doing. Sir Lambegus my cousin, whom you might remember, inherited it. But he died tragically, slain by the night dragons, and it came to me.

It's true that the King of Spain's daughter came across the sea to visit and was fascinated by the nutmeg and the pear and all. That's sometimes what people get reminded of when...

Sir, I am NOT trying to drive all thoughts from your head with idle chatter. I do but try to help you remember. At our age we need all the help we can get.

You recall me as a great traitor who fought at Mordred's side at Camlann, that last battle where he and so many others died and Arthur our King was badly wounded? You slew me with your own hand as I tried to escape, you say? There sir, your memory is at fault as can be said of so many of us after a certain point in our lives.

You're mistaken, sir, if you think I fought against my king and companions. The mead has gotten to you, and I see your eyes closing. I believe you need to return to your slumbers and that when you awaken you'll remember differently.

And there he goes, staggering down the hallway. So many of you silent, floating faces are watching me now! I wonder if Caradoc will remember me again. In fact I never owned a nut tree, magic or otherwise. But there is another verse to that song and it describes me, I think:

I skipped over water
I danced over sea
And all the birds in the air
Couldn't catch me.

My favorite time as a lad was when I was Lord of Misrule, a page boy set upon the throne with the scullery maid beside him in the best bed and the Lord and Lady washing plates in the kitchen. It was a surprise the first time I awoke and found myself here and in this company, but it felt familiar and I knew what to do.

Caradoc is right. I fought on Mordred's side at that last great battle. Everything appeared to be going his way politically. Many others joined Mordred, though I haven't encountered any of them here. If I'd felt that supporting him was an act of courage, I wouldn't have done it.

Certain honorable knights, like Percival, died well before the battle of Camlann. Others, French knights like Bors, weren't there. But Caradoc not only was there, he was the one who slew me with an un-knightly blow to my back as I sought to remove myself from the fight. Even spending my courage as thriftily as I've done, I had very little left by then.

So why am I here? I thought at first that Morgana and her sorceress sisters had mistakenly gathered me up with all the fallen heroes and transported me to this place to await Arthur's awakening.

Now I think that it was done on purpose to entertain you floating heads. That you know me for what I am and that my presence here amuses you.

Lately I don't sleep for more than a few hours at a stretch and wander the halls the rest of the time spreading a certain amount of doubt and jealousy. I'm the fly in the ointment, the dead dog in the well, the sign that any system run by humans will have flaws.

The King is stirring, I can sense that. I go through the Great Hall, up the flight of stone stairs to the Royal chamber. More faces than I can count, more really than I can conceive of, float around me now.

When I enter the chamber still more faces, clouds of them, fill the air. You give no sign of concern about such dire events as might have caused the King to rise and return. In fact you watch Arthur with expressions of interest like people observing a well-matched game of chess, a round of draughts played for moderately high stakes.

Arthur lies as always alone and unattended. His hands and legs move, his eyes open. The first thing he sees is me.

The King does not know fear even when awakening in these strange surrounding. But he does show surprise at the sight of me. I drop to one knee.

"My liege," I say. He looks puzzled at first. "No need for you to remember my name, sire. I am Sir Morgravain."

He nods his head and remembers. His expression says that he recognizes the fly in the ointment. But I will be the first to speak to his majesty, and I will plant my ideas before anyone else can.

You faces watch all this with fascination. I don't know if this is a great event or a great entertainment. But if, as I believe, it's a dash of mischief you want, then I am your own true knight.

Illustration by Gustave Doré for "Idylls of the King" by
Lord Alfred Tennyson, 1868

# The Queen and the Cambion

## 1.

"Silly Billy, The Sailor King," some called King William IV of Great Britain. But never, of course, to his royal face. Then it was always, "Yes, sire," and "As your majesty wishes!"

Because certain adults responsible for her care didn't watch their words in front of a child, the king's young niece and heir to his throne heard such things said. It angered her.

Princess Victoria liked her uncle and knew that King William IV always treated her as nicely as a boozy, confused, former sea captain of a monarch could be expected to, and much of the time rather better.

Often when she greeted him he would lean forward, slip a secret gift into her hands, and whisper something like, "Discovered this in the late King your grandfather's desk at Windsor."

These generally were small items—trinkets, jewels, mementos, long ago tributes from minor potentates that he'd found in the huge half-used royal palaces, stuck in his pocket, and as often as not remembered to give to his niece.

The one she found most fascinating was a piece of very ancient parchment that someone had pressed under glass hundreds of years before. This came into her possession one day when she was twelve as King William passed Victoria and her governess on his way to the royal coach.

His Britannic Majesty paused and said in her ear, "It's a spell, little cub. Put your paw in mine."

Victoria felt something in her hand and slipped it into a pouch under her cloak while the Sailor King lurched by as though he was walking the quarterdeck of a ship in rough water. "Every ruler of this island has had it, and many of us have invoked it," he mumbled while climbing the carriage steps.

She followed him. "To use in times of great danger to Britain?" she whispered.

He leaned out the window. "Or on a day of doldrums and no wind in the sails," he roared as if she was up in a crow's nest, his face red as semi-rare roast beef. "You'll be the monarch and damn all who'd say you no."

Victoria didn't take the gift from under her cloak until she was quite alone in the library of the dark and dreary palace at Kensington. It's where she lived under the intense care of her mother the widowed Duchess of Kent, a German lady, and Sir John Conroy, a handsome enough Irish army officer of good family.

The Duchess had appointed Conroy comptroller of her household. Between them they tried to make sure the princess had no independence at all. Victoria really only got out of their sight when King Billy summoned her to the Royal Court.

Nobody at Kensington ever used the library. She went to the far end of that long room lined with portraits of the obscure daughters and younger sons of various British kings, many with their plump consorts and empty-eyed children. Victoria pushed aside a full length curtain and in the waning daylight looked at the page.

She deciphered a bit of the script and discovered words in Latin, which she knew. She saw the name Arturus, which made her gasp. Other words just seemed to be a collection of letters.

Then for fear that someone was coming she hid it away behind a shelf full of books of sermons by long-dead clergymen. It's where she kept some other secret possessions, for she was allowed very little privacy.

She knew the pronunciation for the Latin. By copying several of the other words and showing them to her language tutor she discovered they were Welsh.

Her music teacher, born in Wales, taught her some pronunciation but became too curious about a few of the words she showed him. Victoria then sought out the old stable master who spoke the language, including some of the ancient tongue, and could read and write a bit.

He was honored and kept her secret when the princess practiced with him. One evening when she had learned all the words and her guardians were busy, Victoria went to the library, took out the page, and slowly read it aloud.

She wasn't quite finished when a silver light shone on the dusty shelves and paintings. Before her was a mountaintop with the sun shining through clouds. In the air, heading her way, sailed a man who rode the wind as another might a horse.

In his hand was the black staff topped with a dragon's head. His grey cloak and robes showed the golden moon in all its phases. His white hair and beard whipped about as the wind brought him to the mountaintop.

At the moment he alighted he noticed Victoria. A look of such vexation came over his face that she stumbled on the words and couldn't immediately repeat them. He and the mountaintop faded from her sight. She, however, remembered what she'd seen.

Victoria was no scholar. But the library at Kensington Palace did contain certain old volumes, and she read all she could find about Arthur and especially about Merlin.

An observant child like Victoria knew John Conroy was more than the Duchess's comptroller. She understood it was his idea to keep her isolated and to have her every move watched. From an early age she knew why.

She heard her uncle tell someone in confidence but with a voice that could carry over wind, waves, and cannon fire, "The mad old man, my father, King George that was, had a coach load and more of us sons. But in the event, only my brother Kent, before he died, produced an heir—fair, square, and legitimate. So the little girl over there stands to inherit the crown when I go under."

If the King did "go under" before she was eighteen, Victoria knew, her mother would be Regent. The Duchess of Kent would control her daughter and the Royal Court, and Conroy would control the Duchess.

In the winter before her eighteenth birthday, five years after he gave her the spell, King William became very ill. But even in sickness, he remembered what the Duchess and Conroy were up to. And though his condition was grave he resolutely refused to die.

On May 24, 1837, Victoria would become eighteen. On May 22 the king was in a coma, and the Duchess and her comptroller had a plan.

From a window of the library at Kensington Palace Victoria saw carriages drive up through a mid-spring drizzle, saw figures in black emerge. She recognized men that Conroy knew: several hungry attorneys, a minor cabinet minister, a rural justice, the secretary of a bishop who believed he should have been an archbishop. They gathered in Conroy's offices downstairs.

Because the servants were loyal, the princess knew that a document had been prepared in which Victoria would cite her own youth and foolishness and beg that her mother (and her mother's "wise advisor") be regent until she was twenty-one.

Even those who admired Victoria would not have said the Princess was brilliant, but neither was she dull or naive. She knew how much damage the conspirators would be able to do in three years of regency. She might never become free. All they needed was her signature.

Understanding what was afoot, Victoria went to the shelf where the manuscript page was hidden. She wondered if she was entitled to do this before she was actually the monarch and if the old wizard would be as angry as the last time.

Victoria heard footsteps on the stairs. She looked at the pictures of her obscure and forgotten ancestors all exiled to the library and made her choice. The door at the other end of the library opened. The Duchess and Conroy entered with half a dozen very solemn men.

"My dearest daughter, we have been trying to decide how best to protect you," said her mother. By the light of three candles Victoria stood firm and recited the Latin, rolled out the Welsh syllables the way she'd been taught.

Duchess and accomplice exchanged glances. Madness was commonplace in the British dynasty. George III had been so mad that a regent had been appointed.

They started towards Victoria then stopped and stared. She turned and saw what they did—a great stone hall lit by shafts of sun through tall windows. The light fell on figures including a big man crowned and sitting on a throne.

Victoria saw again the tall figure in robes adorned with golden moons in all their phases. In his hand was a black staff topped with a dragon's head. This time his hair and beard were iron grey not white. He shot the king a look of intense irritation. The king avoided his stare and seemed a bit amused.

Merlin strode out of the court at Camelot and the royal hall vanished behind him. Under his breath he muttered, "A curse upon the day I was so addled as to make any oath to serve at the beck and call of every half-wit or lunatic who planted a royal behind on the throne of Britain."

Then he realized who had summoned him to this dim and dusty place, and his face softened just a bit. Not a monarch yet to judge by her attire. But soon enough she would be.

Victoria gestured toward the people gaping at him. Merlin was accustomed to those who tried to seize power using bloody axes, not pieces of paper. But a wizard understands the cooing of the dove, the howl of the wolf, and the usurper's greed.

He leveled his staff and blue flames leaped forth.

The documents Conroy held caught fire, and he dropped them. The red wig on one attorney and the ruffled cuffs of the bishop's secretary also ignited. Since none of them would ever admit to having been there none would ever have to describe how they fled, the men snuffing out flames, barely pausing to let the duchess go first.

When they were gone, Merlin erased the fire with a casual wave. Easy enough, he thought. Nothing like Hastings or the Battle of Britain. Shortly he'd be back in Camelot giving the king a piece of his mind.

"Lord Merlin…" the young princess began, "We thank you."

A wizard understands a bee and a queen equally. And both can understand a wizard. Merlin spoke and she heard the word "Majesty" in her head. He dropped to one knee and kissed her hand. For young Victoria this was their first meeting. For Merlin it was not.

Time was a path that crossed itself again and again, and memory could be prophecy. Later in her life, earlier in his, this queen would summon him.

He had a certain affection for her. But in his lifetime he'd already served all four of the Richards, five or six of the Henry's, the first Elizabeth, the ever-tiresome Ethelred, Saxon Harold, Norman William, and a dozen others.

He waited for her to dismiss him. But Victoria said in a rush of words, "I read that you are a cambion born of Princess Gwenddydd by the incubus Albercanix. She became a nun after your birth." The princess was enthralled.

Merlin met her gaze, gave the quick smile a busy adult has for a child. One trick that always distracted monarchs was to show how they came to have power over such a one as he.

The wizard waved his hand, and Victoria saw the scene after Mount Badon, the great victory that made Arthur king of Britain. That day Merlin ensorcelled seven Saxon wizards, Arthur slew seven Saxon kings and may well have saved his sorcerer's life.

For this princess Merlin mostly hid the gore away. He showed her Arthur and himself younger, flushed with victory and many cups of celebratory mead as in gratitude the wizard granted the king any wish within his power to give.

"Neither of us knew much law so it wasn't well thought out," he explained and showed himself swearing an oath to come forever more to the aid of any monarch of Britain who summoned him. "But my time is precious and must not be wasted," he told her.

Even this mild version left Victoria round eyed with wonder, as was Merlin's intent. For certain monarchs his message could be so clear and terrifying that Richard III had gone to his death on Bosworth Field and Charles I had let his head be whacked off without trying to summon him.

For a moment wizard and princess listened and smiled at the sounds downstairs of carriages fleeing into the night.

He bowed, asked if there was anything more she desired. When she could think of nothing he bowed once more, stepped backwards through the bookshelves and the wall of Kensington Palace.

She watched as the great hall of the castle with its knights and king appeared and swallowed up Merlin.

## 2.

"I am ruled by our young queen and happily so, as is every man of fair mind in this land," said Lord Melbourne, Queen Victoria's first Prime Minister. And for a brief time that was true.

Melbourne could be a bit of a wizard, producing parliamentary majorities out of nothing, or making them disappear without a trace. A few years into young Victoria's reign, gossip held she was in the palm of his hand.

In fact she found him charming, but with her mother left behind at Kensington Palace and John Conroy exiled to the Continent, the headstrong young queen was led by no one.

The dusty castles and palaces in London and Windsor had lately been the haunts of drunken and sometimes deranged kings. She opened them up and gathered visiting European princes and her own young equerries and ladies-in-waiting for late-night feasts and dances.

Then Lord Melbourne explained to her that the people of Britain were unhappy with their monarch. "The time has come," he said, "for you to find a husband, produce an heir, and ensure stability. The choice of a groom will be yours, an opportunity and a peril. Like every marriage."

Victoria's first reaction was anger. But she knew that few women of any rank got to choose their husbands. Her choices were wide. The eligible princes of Europe paraded through Buckingham Palace and Windsor Castle. Victoria and the Grand Duke Alexander of Russia danced the wild mazurka. Young equerries of her staff had her picture on lockets next to their hearts in the hope that she might decide to marry into her nobility and select one of them.

The nation was fascinated with its legendary past, and so was its queen. She dreamed of sending the candidates on quests, having them do great deeds. But she knew that wasn't possible.

Victoria's resentment of the task made her unable to decide among the candidates. Naturally, everyone grew impatient—the potential grooms, the government, and the people of England.

As the situation worsened, the Queen considered invoking Merlin, but she felt intimidated. Then Melbourne himself said the future of Britain hung on her decision. She thought this surely was a moment to summon the wizard.

One evening in her private chambers she drew out the parchment and ran through the invocation. Immediately the light of the oil lamps in her room was drowned by sunlight shining on ocean waves, pouring through windows of clearest glass into a room blue as the sea around it.

Despite his robes with the golden moon in all its phases, it took her a few moments to recognize the tall figure with dark hair and beard standing over a giant tortoise that rested on an oaken table. Victoria watched fascinated as he stopped what he was doing and said good-by effusively but quickly to a figure with liquid green eyes and saucy silver back flippers. The Sea King's Daughter and her palace disappeared as he strode into Victoria's private drawing room.

Merlin in the full flush of his wizardry had just murmured, "Gryphons and Guilfoils, marjoram and unicorn mange, the heart of Diana's own rabbit soaked in the blood of humming birds from the Emperor's gardens in far Cathay…"

Then he'd felt the summons, turned, seen Victoria, and lost track of the spell he was working. But a summons when it came had to be obeyed. It could originate at any point in the long history of British monarchy from the battle of Badon on. And each caught him at a moment in his life when he was deep into weaving magic and casting spells. At his most powerful he was at his most vulnerable.

He stepped out of a place where each drinking cup had a name and every chair an ancestry into a room with walls covered by images of flowers and pictures of bloodless people. The floor was choked with furniture, and every single surface was covered with myriad small objects.

Merlin had encountered Victoria when he was just a youth and she was middle aged. That meeting would, of course, not have happened to her yet. Now in her private apartments at Windsor Palace he knelt before Victoria

119

whose expression was full of curiosity about the tortoise, the palace, the creature with the flippers, and him.

But what she said was, "I brought you here because my prime minister and my people have decided I must marry for the good of Britain. I need your help to make the right decision."

And he told her as patiently as he could, "In the Palace of the Sea King's Daughter, as an act of charity I was working a spell to restore the zest of life to an ancient tortoise. It houses within itself the soul of Archimedes, the great mage of legendary times. This is the sort of favor I hope someone might someday perform if I ever needed it.

"It was all about to come together: ingredients at hand, incantation memorized, pentagrams and quarter circles drawn, the tortoise staring up with hope in its eyes."

She sat amazed by this and by the man, dark-bearded and thirty years younger than when she'd seen him a few years before. Victoria dreamed of turning her kingdom into a kind of Camelot, a land of castles, enchanted woods, knights in armor, and maidens under sleeping spells floating down rivers. She looked at Merlin now and thought of how perfectly he would fit into such a world.

Merlin understood. He was young, vain, and used to being wanted. He found himself liking, her but memories of the complications and quarrels after an extended tumble with Elizabeth I reminded him of how unwise such liaisons could be. His interest at the moment was getting back as quickly as possible to the life he'd had to leave.

Victoria watched him stand at the floor-length windows and stare out into the night. When he gestured, one window blew open.

Any wizard is a performer, and Merlin intended to bedazzle her. He held out his right arm, candlelight danced, and a bird appeared. The shadow of a raptor rested on his wrist and seemed to flicker like a flame.

Merlin had summoned a questing spirit, the ghost of the Lord of Hawks. He whistled a single note, and it became solid, all angry, unblinking eyes and savage beak.

The wizard filled a clear crystal bowl with water and said, "Your majesty, give me the name of a suitor."

She named the Grand Duke Alexander of Russia. Merlin held the hawk near the bowl, which was so clear that the water seemed to float in air. He whispered the grand duke's name and looked at the surface of the water. On it he saw Alexander's fate, a winter scene with blood on the snow. An anarchist had hurled the bomb that tore the Tsar apart.

Merlin knew Victoria was not a vicious soul. If she saw this particular piece of the future it would be hard for her to keep it a secret from the Tsar-to-be. And it was best not to upset the balance of the world. Undoing that would require more magic than he had.

So he looked at the young queen and shook his head—this one was not suitable. She looked but he had already cleared away the image.

"Who is your majesty's next suitor?"

Victoria spoke the name, Merlin relayed it to his medium, and the image of a mildly retarded prince of Savoy floated in the bowl. He shook his head, she looked relieved, and they ran through some more European royalty. Merlin knew the man he was looking for, the one she actually had married. He'd seen pictures galore at that time in her future and his past when he'd been summoned by this queen.

She stared at Merlin as she smiled and said, "Lord Alfred Paget." This was the most dashing of her young courtiers. A royal equerry of excellent family, he made no secret of his romantic love for his queen. She in turn was charmed and more than a bit taken with Paget. He would be her choice if she decided to marry one not of royal birth.

But Merlin knew that wasn't the name he was looking for. When an image floated on the water, it actually made Merlin grin. He let Victoria see the once dashing Paget fat, self-satisfied, and seventy years old.

"Oh dear. This will not do!" she said with a horrified expression. Then she and the wizard laughed.

This search for a husband was far more pleasant than much of what he did in service to the Baden oath. Merlin had seen an unfaithful royal princess killed in Paris by flashing lights and a willful, runaway machine. He had visited a distant time when the king of Britain was not much more than a picture that moved.

Victoria gave the name and title of Albert Prince of Saxe-Coburg and Gotha. A glance at the face floating on the water was all Merlin needed. This was the one he'd been waiting for.

Albert would die long before Victoria did, and she would mourn him for the rest of her life. A hardier husband might be in order. But Albert was the one she was destined to marry, and that's how it would be. The image floating in the bowl was flattering. Merlin invited the queen to look, indicated his approval, and congratulated her.

His task done, Merlin prepared to leave. Victoria realized this and looked stricken.

Anyone, be they human or cambion, enjoys being found attractive. And to have won the heart of a queen was better still. Merlin bowed deeply to the monarch and wished her great happiness in her marriage.

As he strode out of her presence Victoria saw the tortoise that contained the soul of Archimedes and the sun dancing on the waves outside the palace and the lovely daughter of the one who rules the tides. The queen noted every detail and wondered if her kingdom could ever contain anything so beautiful. She wrote a letter to Prince Albert of Saxe-Coburg and Gotha as she thought of Merlin.

3.

"Twenty-five years into her reign, her Majesty has abandoned her responsibilities."

"Since poor Prince Albert died, I hear she wears nothing but mourning clothes…"

"The processes of government demand the public presence of a monarch."

"…and talks to the trees at Windsor Palace, like her daft grandfather did…"

"No one in her royal household, her government, and especially her family dares to broach the subject to her."

"…curtsies to them trees as well, I got told."

Isolated as a monarch is, Victoria heard the nonsense her people were saying. She knew they said she talked to her late husband as she walked the halls of Buckingham

Palace and Windsor Castle, of Balmoral in Scotland and Osborn House on the Isle of Wight.

And here they were right, sometimes she did. More than anything else what she had lost with the death of the man to whom she'd been married for twenty years was the one person in Britain who could speak to her as an equal. She still spoke to him, but there was no reply. She felt utterly alone.

At Osborn House, after a day with little warmth in the sun, she stood at a window with a wind coming in from the sea and thought of Merlin. Indeed with its graceful Italianate lines, fountains, and views of the water, Osborn was Victoria's attempt to evoke the glimpses she'd caught of the palace of the Sea King's Daughter. She envied that royal family as she did no other.

In the years of her marriage she sometimes remembered the handsome wizard of their last meeting, always with a pang of guilt. It almost felt as if she had betrayed the marriage. In her widowhood, though, she thought about him more often.

That evening at Osborn, Victoria demanded she be completely alone in her private apartments. The queen debated with herself as to whether this was a time of danger to the crown or, as her uncle had said, a day of doldrums and no wind in the sails.

Victoria finally decided it was a good deal of both. She took the glass-bound page out of its hiding place and read the summons aloud. Immediately she saw half-naked people in savage garb looking up at a huge picture that moved. It showed some kind of carriage without horses racing down a dark, smooth road.

As monarch of a forward-looking nation the queen had been shown zoetropes and magic lanterns. This appeared far more like real life, except that it moved too fast. Her royal train was always an express, and its engine could attain speeds of almost fifty miles an hour. But that was as nothing to what this machine seemed to do.

A man, who looked familiar, like a distant cousin perhaps, sat in it smiling. "In this driver's seat everyone is a king," he said.

The queen couldn't know that she'd just had a glimpse of a distant successor. In the year 2159 King Henry X had on a permanent loop in his offices what he called "My Agincourt." The great triumph of his reign was being named spokesperson for Chang'an/Ford/Honda, the world's mightiest auto maker.

Victoria saw that the people who had been looking up at the image were now frozen, staring at a figure running straight toward her.

This one had long dark hair but no sign of a beard, was tall but not quite as tall as the Merlin she remembered. He looked very young. Instead of robes he wore what Victoria identified as some abbreviated form of men's underclothes, a thing about which she made a point of knowing nothing. As he stepped into her room she saw emblazoned on the shirt the lion and the unicorn, the royal crest, directly over his heart.

Victoria had sons, and she placed this boy as fifteen at most. She stared at him and said, "You're just a child. Who are you? Where are your proper clothes? And how did you get here?"

Merlin after a moment of surprise looked this small woman in black directly in the eyes, which none had done since Albert. Victoria heard him say, "I am Merlin the cambion of Albercanix and Gwenddydd. I was apprenticed to Galapas, the Hermit of the Crystal Cave, a disagreeable old tyrant.

"One morning running through my spells, I found myself summoned by Henry X, king of Britain. I was working a great magic on his courtiers when you called me here."

He glanced down at the soft clothes and shoes that still puzzled him, "And this is the livery of that king." He seemed confused.

When the young wizard first arrived in 2159, King Henry peered at him over a glass and said, "Not what I expected. Just curious as to whether this old piece of parchment actually worked—needed something to remind myself and others of the old mystique of royalty. Perhaps you could turn a few advertising people into mice. It'll teach them to respect me and the monarchy in its last days."

Victoria saw in this somewhat lost and gangling lad the man she'd encountered. The Queen realized that King Arthur and the Baden Oath were well in his future and that he didn't understand what had happened to him. It occurred to her that the child of a demon and a princess who became a nun might be as separate and alone as she was.

"Your attire simply won't do," she said.

Merlin discovered that unlike King Henry, this monarch was greatly respected. All the servants deferred to her and some courtiers were even afraid.

The queen had a trusted footman and pageboy dress this stranger in clothes her sons had outgrown. Merlin hated the infinite buttons and hooks, the itching flannel and stiff boots.

Victoria passed him off as a young visiting kinsman, "From the Anhalt-Latvia cousins."

Merlin remembered King Henry, so full of strange potions and drinks he sometimes had trouble standing and often couldn't remember who Merlin was. The young wizard had tried not to show how bedazzled he was by the magic of that court, lights that came and went with the wave of a hand, cold air that seeped out of walls to cool a kingdom where it was always hot outdoors, unseen musicians who beat drums, sang, played harps of incredible variety through the day and night without tiring.

The king's entourage was so amazed by Merlin's spells of invisibility and the way he could turn them into frogs and back into courtiers that they lost any interest in their monarch and flocked around him. They persuaded Merlin to surrender his own rough robes and gave him shorts, t-shirts, and soft shoes like everyone else in the kingdom. He had never worn clothes with legs or felt fabric as light.

All he knew for certain was that he didn't want to return to the Crystal Cave and the Hermit. He spent some amazing days and light-filled nights in the court of 2159.

Victoria, everyone agreed, seemed more cheerful since the appearance of her strange relative. The two of them took walks together, and he showed her nixies riding in on the morning waves and sprites dancing by moonlight. He turned her pug dog into a trained bear and turned it back again.

Merlin didn't understand this world in which palaces and castles all looked utterly indefensible, ruins had been built just to be ruins, and the queen's knights seemed an unlikely band of warriors without a missing eye or gouged-out nose among them.

On their walks Victoria sometimes ran on about wanting to create a court full of art and poetry like King Arthur at Camelot. It amazed her that he understood none of this. So she told him the bits and pieces she had learned over the years about the Baden Oath and Arthur's kingdom. The young mage was fascinated.

Once she made Merlin sit through a chamber music concert and talked afterwards about "the melodies of the wonderful Herr Mendelssohn to whom I could listen forever." He told her about the court of her descendent Henry X where invisible musicians played all day and all night.

He could have told her more about the future of her kingdom. But out of respect and even affection he never much mentioned her descendant. Never described seeing King Henry in a false crown, armor, and broadsword quaff "Royal English Ale" from a horn cup and signify his approval. Never said how he'd sampled the ale and found it so vile he spat it out.

When he'd finished that endorsement the king had turned and seen the shocked expression on young Merlin's face. He said, "I'm the last, you know. I'm preserved in so many formats that they'll never need another king for their ads. I've no children that I know of and no one is interested in succeeding me. I'm sorry I let you see all this." He started to cry great drunken tears.

Merlin walked away as quickly as he could. He strode into the room where his majesty's greatest promotional moments played on a screen. He didn't know where he was going, but he headed for a door and the blazing hot outdoors.

When some of His Majesty's courtiers tried to stop him he froze them in place with a spell. At that moment of his magic Victoria's summons rescued him.

For that and her stories he would always be grateful. But he was young, male, and a wizard, and this was a queen's court with many young women without much to do.

Merlin knew little about such things. But others did. There was a fine rumpus of a rendezvous in a linen closet with an apprentice maid of the wardrobe and another more leisurely meeting with a young lady-in-waiting in her chamber.

Spells to blank the memories of passersby didn't quite dispel the stories. The queen found out about it and knew it was her fault. Even Albert, as good a man as has ever lived, had more animal in him than was reasonable or necessary. Keeping Merlin here was as unnatural as imprisoning a wild beast. And now there would be anxious months spent waiting to find out if the grandchild of an incubus had been spawned at the Royal Court. She ordered certain clothing to be made.

One day Merlin returned to his rooms and found on the bed robes and a cloak with the moon in all its phases and fine leather boots like the ones Her Majesty had noticed older Merlins wearing.

The youth had never seen anything so splendid. He changed and went to her private rooms where she was waiting. "Sir Merlin, you have fulfilled and more the tasks for which you were summoned," she said, and he saw how hard this was for her. "You are dismissed with our thanks and the certainty we will meet again."

Merlin bowed low. And before the royal tears came, or his own could start, he found himself hurtling backwards through the centuries to the hermit Galapas and the Crystal Cave.

Merlin didn't linger there but immediately set out across Wales, finding within himself the magic to cover miles in minutes. One story Victoria had told was of a king trying to build a castle before his enemies were upon him. Each day the walls would be raised, and each night they would be thrown down. All were in despair until a bold youth in a cloak of moons appeared. He tamed two dragons that fought every night in the caves below the castle and made the walls collapse. Merlin knew he was that youth.

## 4.

"Queen Victoria," a commentator said at her Golden Jubilee, "Inherited a Britain linked by stage coach and reigned in a Britain that ran on rails. She ruled over a quarter of the globe and a quarter of its people."

At Balmoral Castle in the Highlands, late in her reign, the queen went into high mourning because a game-keeper, John Brown, had died.

"Mrs. Brown mourns dead husband," was how a scurrilous underground London sheet put it.

In fact Brown—belligerent, hard-drinking, and rude to every person at court except Her Majesty—was the only one on earth who spoke to her as one human being to another. He died unmourned by anyone but the queen. But she mourned him extravagantly. Memorial plaques were installed; statuettes were manufactured.

He was gone but the court's relief was short lived. To commemorate becoming Empress of India, Victoria imported servants from the subcontinent. Among them was Abdul Karim who taught her a few words of Hindu. For this the queen called him "the Munshi," or teacher, and appointed him her private secretary. Soon the Munshi was brought along to state occasions, allowed to handle secret government reports, introduced to foreign dignitaries. He engaged in minor intrigue and told her majesty nasty stories about his fellow servants.

The entire court wished the simple, straight-forward Mr. Brown back. Victoria's children, many well into middle-age, found the Munshi appalling. The government worried about its state secrets.

"Indian cobra in Queen's parlor," the slander sheets proclaimed.

The queen would hear nothing against him. But she knew he wasn't what she wanted.

❧

"Oh the cruelty of young women and the folly of old men," Merlin cried as he paced the floor in the tower of glass that was his prison cell.

Nimue the enchantress who beguiled his declining years had turned against him, used the skills he'd taught her to imprison him.

As a boy Queen Victoria had told him about King Uther Pendragon, whose castle walls collapsed each night. Solving that, young Merlin won the confidence of Pendragon. The birth of the king's son Arthur, hiding the infant from usurpers, the sword in the stone, the kingdom of Britain, and all the rest had followed from that.

But Victoria never told Merlin about Nimue. She thought it too sad.

"Sired by an incubus, baptized in church, tamer of dragons, advisor to kings, I am a cambion turned into a cuckold," he wailed.

Most of his magic had deserted him. He hadn't even enough to free himself. Still he did little spells, turned visiting moths into butterflies, made his slippers disappear and reappear. Merlin knew he had a reason for doing this but couldn't always remember what it was.

Then one morning while making magic he found himself whisked from the tower and summoned to a room crammed full of tartan pillows with claymore swords hung on the walls as decoration. Music played in the next room, and an old lady in black looked at him kindly.

The slump of his shoulders, the unsteadiness of his stance, led the Queen of England, the Empress of India, to rise and lead him over to sit on the divan next to her. "That music you hear is a string quartet playing a reduction of Herr Mendelssohn's Scottish Symphony," she said. "Musicians are on call throughout my waking hours. You told me long ago this was how things were arranged at the Royal Court in 2159."

It was a brisk day, and they drank mulled wine. "The sovereign of Britain requires a wizard to attend Her," she said, "for a period of time which She shall determine."

Merlin realized he was rescued. And when the Munshi walked into the room unannounced, the Wizard stood to his full height. Seeing a white-bearded man with flashing eyes and sparks darting from his hands, the Munshi fled.

Everyone at Balmoral marveled at the day her Majesty put aside her secretary and gave orders that he was not to approach her. All wondered if someone else had taken his place, but no evidence of that could ever be found.

People talked about the eccentricities of Queen Victoria's last years: the seat next to hers that she insisted always be kept empty in carriages, railroad cars, at state dinners, the rooms next to hers that must never be entered.

At times the queen would send all the ladies and servants away from her chambers and not let them in until next morning.

Some at court hinted that all this had shaded over into madness and attributed it to heredity. Most thought it was just old age, harmless, and in its way charmingly human.

In fact a few members of her court did see things out of the corners of their eyes. Merlin could conjure invisibility, but his concentration was no longer perfect.

Her majesty walking over the gorse at Balmoral in twilight, on the shore on a misty day at Osborn, in the corridors of Windsor Castle would suddenly be accompanied by a cloaked figure with a white beard and long white hair. When the viewer looked again he would have disappeared. Those who saw thought it best not to mention it to anyone.

She talked to Merlin about their prior meetings and how she cherished each of them. The wizard would once have sneered at the picturesque ruins and the undefendable faux castles that dotted the landscape near any royal residence. Now he understood they had been built in tribute to the sage who'd saved the young princess, the handsome magician who had helped choose her husband, the quicksilver youth of her widowhood.

When she finally became very ill at Windsor, Queen Victoria had been ruling for over sixty years. Merlin remembered that this was the time when she would die. He stayed with her, put in her mind the things he knew she found pleasing, summoned up music only she could hear. He wondered if, when she was gone, he would be returned to Nimue and the tower.

"She assumed the throne in the era of Sir Walter Scott and her reign has lasted into the century of Mr. H.G. Wells," the Times of London said.

In the last days when her family came to see her, Victoria had the glass with the parchment inside it under her covers. Merlin stood in a corner and was visible only to the Queen.

When her son who would be Edward VII appeared, Merlin shook his head. This man would never summon him. It was the same with her grandson who would be George V. A great-grandchild, a younger son who stammered was brought in with his brothers. Merlin nodded: this one would summon him to London decades later when hellfire fell from the skies.

The boy was called back after he and his brothers had left, was given the parchment and shown how to hide it.

"You are my last and only friend," Victoria told Merlin. He held her hands when she died and felt grief for the first time in his life. But he wasn't returned to his glass prison. Uninvited, invisible, utterly alone at the funeral, he followed the caisson that bore the coffin through the streets of Windsor, carrying the only friend he'd ever had to the Royal Mausoleum at Frogmore.

"We say of certain people, 'She was a woman of her time,'" an orator proclaimed. "But of how many can it be said that the span of their years, the time in which they lived, will be named for them?"

"A bit of her is inside each one of us," said a woman watching the cortege. "And that I suppose is what a legend is."

In the winter twilight with snow on the ground, Merlin stood outside the mausoleum. "I don't want to transfer my mind and soul to another human or beast, and I won't risk using that magic and getting summoned. There's no other monarch I wish to serve."

He remembered the Hermit of the Crystal Cave. Old Galapas hadn't been much of a teacher, but Merlin had learned the Wizard's Last Spell from him. It was simple enough, and he hadn't forgotten. Merlin invoked it, and those who had lingered in the winter dusk saw for a moment a figure with white hair and beard, wearing robes with the moon in all its phases.

The old wizard waved a wand, shimmered for a moment, then appeared to shatter. In the growing dark what seemed like tiny stars flew over the mausoleum, over Windsor, over Britain, and all the world.

Illustration by Gustave Doré, frontpiece, for *Perrault's Fairy Tales (Les Contes de Perrault)*, 1867

# A Secret History of Small Books

1

It's said that Charles Perrault with one very short book, *Histoires et Contes de Temps Passé*, in 1697 established the Fairy Tale as a literary form. Possibly he also established the validity of the short book of Fairy Tales.

To an oral tradition upheld by women handing down stories from one generation to another, Perrault added elegance and ironic morals. Fairy Tales became reading matter for the Royal Court.

It also became a genre dominated, as the original tales had been, by women, though now these were aristocrats. They brought subtlety of motive and depth of feeling to the form. De Beaumont's "Beauty and the Beast" and other stories were aimed at children. But many others, including d'Alnoy, author of "The Bluebird," intended their stories for adults. The form was a disguise, serious themes concealed in toys.

The French Fairy Tale began with one small book. The massive forty-one volume collection *Le Cabinet des Fées* (1785-1789) was its culmination. The Revolution of

1789 ended the world in which it had flourished. Maybe only Perrault himself could have found the perfect ironic moral for this story.

In the small book you hold in your hands, "Seven Smiles and Six Frowns" is a tale about the evolution of a Fairy Tale; "The Cinnamon Cavalier" is a Fairy Tale variation that has been called by a critic "The Gingerbread Man, writ large"; "The Margay's Children" is a modern take on a "Beastly Bridegroom" story: everyone has animal ancestors after all.

## 2

In the nineteenth century the Brothers Grimm aimed their Folk/Fairy tales at both adults and children. During the same period the short story arose as a literary form. Many of the authors who created it—Irving, Hoffmann, Poe, Gogol, etc.—wrote for adults and wrote fantasy, sometimes a lot of it.

In this new genre, writers often took the Fairy Tale and gave it literary purpose. Small books had a place here unlike their hold on any other prose form. Andersen's Fairy Tales originally came out in tiny collections, five or six stories at a time. Perhaps it's those beginnings that make Eva Le Gallienne's Andersen translation with Sendak illustrations, *Seven Tales by H.C. Andersen* from 1958, seem right and proper and new. It gives some of the feel of what it may have been like to discover Andersen in those original little volumes.

Oscar Wilde was his successor, creating, like Andersen, characters who know loneliness and alienation. His two fairy tale collections, *The Happy Prince* and *The House of Pomegranates,* between them are just nine stories. Short and bittersweet, they constitute a major part of his published short fiction.

The sadly neglected Barbara Leonie Picard admired Andersen and Wilde. She established her career in the mid-twentieth century with three good sized books of fine, original Fairy Tales. But my favorite of hers is *The Goldfinch Garden,* seven tales left out of the earlier compilations. In little more than a hundred small pages her stories of mismatched lovers, the search for friendship, and the fate of magic creatures in the human world have an intimacy the longer collections do not.

Arguably, these books with their bright covers and illustrations are short because they're intended for children. There is truth in that. But the French wrote mainly for adults. Andersen's stories found an adult audience and then a huge child audience. Wilde's stories were intended for children and adults who read to them or to themselves.

In 1938 Margaret Yourcenar, author of *The Memoirs of Hadrian,* first woman member of the French Academy, produced *Oriental Tales.* She took the basic European Fairy Tale trope and rang upon it eleven ingenious and original changes in perhaps twenty-eight thousand words.

It has no illustrations, and one can't say for certain that no child has read it in the decades since it was first published. But I think its life is a testimony to that secret group: adult Fairy Tale readers.

Of the writers I've mentioned who followed the Grimms, Picard was a recluse, and about her we can only conjecture. But the others were lesbian or gay. Perhaps all found a refuge in Fairy Tales, a woman's art form in a straight male world. As with the French women, I think there's a hint of camouflage in these stories. The authors create alternate worlds in which they can describe the consequences of their own loneliness, poverty, and alienation, and can even imagine happy endings. These subjects rendered realistically, especially the sexual aspects, would put off and even offend readers in the nineteenth and early twentieth centuries. Fairy Tales and the Fantasy genre that descends from them show a reality that is and is not the one we live in. For LGBT children and adults that divergence is familiar ground as it was for feminist writers like Carter and Sexton who used the tropes in their work.

In this collection, I'd classify as genre fantasy "The Progress of Solstice and Chance," with its complex sexual relations and invented pantheon of gods, the outrageous situation and characters of "The Bear Dresser's Secret," and the introduction of noir detective themes into a Fairy Kingdom in "The Lady of Wands."

## 3.

Like those of the girl in my "Seven Frowns and Seven Smiles," my parents could be indulgent. As a small child I heard stories from The Thurber Carnival such as "The Day the Dam Broke" or "The Night the Ghost Got In," as my bedtime reading. But I also had the *Arabian Nights* and Doctor Dolittle and King Arthur for company.

I learned the Arthurian Matter of Britain wasn't a Fairy Tale but a legend, which to me meant colorful backgrounds and lots of detail. I was given *The Once and Future King* soon after it came out. The sexual underpinnings of the story were a revelation. My fascination with stuff like this was one of the many things best keep hidden in 1960 Boston. Not long after I read it, *Camelot*, the Broadway bound musical adaptation of the book, tried out in town. I was sixteen and in my senior year. I skipped school, slipped into the standing room at a Wednesday matinee, was bedazzled by the show—and caught by my mother who was also in the audience. I was severely grounded. A week or two later when I was allowed my freedom I passed by the Colonial theater on a drizzly late autumn afternoon. The *Camelot* company had gone on to New York but in the alley next to the theater were the sodden remains of Nimue's marvelous green and silver castle.

In the very long show as it was seen out of town, this was where she seduced and imprisoned Merlin. That scene was dropped in Boston. The castle, broken into parts but still recognizable, sat waiting for Callahan Carting to haul it away.

I stood for a long while staring at this wrecked fragment of my secret world. Water ran down the turrets. No one can see tears in twilight in the rain. Here was magic and the end of magic all in one.

"Sir Morgravain Speaks of Night Dragons and Other Things" and "The Queen and the Cambion," were written for that kid.

Illustration by Gustave Doré, "Puss in boots" ("Le chat botté"), for *Perrault's Fairy Tales (Les Contes de Perrault)*, 1867

## About the Author

Richard Bowes has published five novels, two short story collections, and over sixty stories. He has won two World Fantasy Awards, an International Horror Guild and, a Million Writers Award. Forthcoming are a reprint of *Minions of the Moon* his Lambda Award Winning Gay Fantasy novel, a new novel in stories *Dust Devil on a Quiet Street*, and a short story collection, *If Angels Fight*.

Made in the USA
Middletown, DE
01 August 2022

70344941R00094